Twisted Love

Lucie Riley

All characters in this publication are fictitious and any resemblance to real persons, living or dead is purely coincidental.

ISBN-13: 9789769556706
ISBN-10: 976955670X

Email: camella@sunbeach.net

Dedication

To those who have confronted and condemned the inexplicable injustices and inhumane acts committed on those who are vulnerable, innocent and helpless.

Contents

1

The Crime

"Here's a news bulletin.

Church Deacon, Jason Matthew, was found dead today at his home. He had stab wounds all over his body.

Foul play is suspected. Police have arrested his adopted son, Simon Carter, for questioning."

The bellowing voice of the male announcer was heard over the radio. The theme from the Isaac Haynes' classic album, *Shaft*, ended the announcement.

"What!" exclaimed Sally Preston. She was astounded. She dropped the magazine she had begun to read on the floor and rushed to the window; the louvres were already opened. She peeped her head through and shouted to her husband Peter, who was tidying up in the garden.

"Peter! Peter!" she screamed through the opened window. "Is your radio on? Did you hear Deacon Matthew has been killed?"

Peter looked up when he heard his wife shout his name, and indicated with a nod that he had heard.

"May he rest in peace," she declared.

She thought about the Deacon and the last time she was with him in his tiny office. They had been discussing the date and venue for the next charity event; she had been tired so had yawned. He had smiled and said,

"Let's discuss this tomorrow."

Sally was about to protest but he raised his hand to his lips and whispered,

"Sssssssssshhhhhhhh. Tomorrow is good enough. I worked you too hard today."

The Deacon then walked towards the door and before he closed it, he turned back to face her, looked at his watch, smiled and said,

"Besides I have to visit Mrs King and I'm already late."

Sally's heart was now pumping very hard. Tears were welling in her eyes as she recalled his last words to her.

How could anyone kill such a good man? She thought.

She made the sign of the cross, touching her forehead, her chest and her shoulders with the tip of her right forefinger, and said aloud: "I always thought that boy was no good."

She watched her husband for any comment or some sign of regret in his demeanour. However, he said nothing. He just turned away and with the back of his baldhead gleaming in the morning sunlight, continued to remove weeds from the vegetable beds.

That's typical of him, especially lately, she thought, looking at his bent back.

Before he had turned, she had seen his mouth moving as though he was muttering to himself.

"So much for being a man of few words," she said aloud.

She hated it when her husband behaved like this. It has become worse of late. He was increasingly distracted and uninterested in what was happening in the family. It had been months now since they had been intimate. She knew that sometimes she had been too tired but he had even stopped the pleading that normally took place before she eventually gave in.

Her friends thought her lucky as she had a husband who knew the "economy of words." She shrugged her shoulders. She was irritated and unimpressed with his lack of response.

There was no indication in his manner that he felt any regret. He should have, because Deacon Matthew had achieved so much since he was assigned to their district, especially with the young people. He also gave their son free piano lessons. He should show some gratitude for that.

Sally had noticed a change in her husband recently. He had employed a new clerical assistant; that used to be Sally job, but she had decided to stop working in their business. She could not handle working there full-time whilst also being secretary to the Deacon who had expanded his outreach programmes in the parish. She therefore now worked solely with the Deacon.

Earlier, she had trained to be a nurse but Peter had begged her to give it up when they started their own business. He had, therefore, not taken her decision to leave the business very well, as he felt that that should be her first priority. She knew, of course, that he didn't understand that spreading the word of the Lord and getting the Catholics who had strayed from the church, to return was equally, if not more, important.

Peter had advertised and employed someone whom she had met only once and that was only after he had already employed her. Sally had not been involved in the interview process. When she was introduced to Trina Daley, she had wanted to laugh out loud; Trina simply didn't seem to fit the role. Sally thought that Trina looked more like someone who should be working in a house of ill repute and not as the madam. She joked about it with Peter, but he assured her that Trina was very good at the job.

His transformation then began. He started spending a lot of money on new clothes. Sally had been accustomed to buying them, or giving an opinion on what was best for a particular occasion. However, he now took on this role himself, explaining that she was far too busy and that he didn't want to bother her. He also told her that he had arranged for his sister in the States to send clothes over. Additionally, he shaved his head and dyed his beard.

Early one Saturday morning, he had left the house, simply saying that he was going to the barber and that he would be home late. Sally was therefore surprised when he walked in later – his head was shaved and an eighteen-carat diamond earring adorned his pierced left ear lobe.

She remembered simply staring, unable to get the words out that were on her mind. Their two boys looked at him, slapped their hands together and told him how good he looked. When she phoned their eldest child, Susan, she had just laughed and told Sally that she too should get a makeover.

"You don't want him looking younger than you, Mom. Don't forget. There are a lot of young women out there looking for a mature man."

"What do you mean?" Sally had asked annoyed. "He needs to act his age."

Now she took the opportunity to reflect on that conversation as she watched her husband as he continued his weed, seemingly indifferent and unaffected by the news of the Deacon's demise.

"Who's going to want him but me? He's an old man." She muttered and turned away from the window before reaching for her telephone, because there were far more important things to talk about than Peter and his transformation.

She knew there were others who would want to discuss what had happened to their beloved Deacon. Before she could pick it up, the phone began to ring.

Sally would have been surprised; Peter was thinking to himself about the sudden death, but his views were very different from his wife's. He believed that the Deacon had treated the young man he had adopted as a personal slave. He would beat Simon constantly and Peter felt it was a shame that no one else had wanted to adopt him. He wished that he could have done so himself, but he had three children and unfortunately was not able to support another.

Peter had witnessed some of this ill-treatment. He remembered on one occasion that the boy had not put out any prayer books; the Deacon had therefore ordered him to bend over a table in the room. The most humiliating part of it was that he had pulled down Simon's trousers and beat him on the buttocks with a leather belt.

This was not done in private; it was done in front of his men's group. All the men had pleaded with the Deacon to give the boy a chance. However, the Deacon still beat. Afterwards, he said that Simon needed to learn to do as he was told. Peter also found out that on that particular night Simon went to bed hungry as part of the punishment. Based on other conversations, he knew that this was not unusual.

On another occasion, Peter witnessed the Deacon angrily kicking the leg of the chair that Simon was sitting on, which caused the boy to fall over: there was no explanation of exactly what he had done to deserve that kind of treatment.

Most of the men in the group had tales to tell of the Deacon's brutality and savagery towards Simon. One of them told of a time when he had gone to the house to do some repairs and witnessed the Deacon pulling Simon by his ear up the steps towards the front door.

Peter knew he could never express his views about the Deacon to his wife or any of the women in the church as they would not believe him. He knew that Sally and the other women believed in everything that the Deacon did and said. He could do no wrong in their eyes. "After all he's God's messenger," he'd heard his wife say after one of the parishioners had criticised the Deacon.

Deacon Matthew arrived in the village about six years previously, apparently from England. The villagers treated him like a demigod. Therefore, Peter knew that if he exposed the Deacon's true nature it would upset them. So, he never told them what he had seen or heard.

"However, if Simon did kill him, that's another thing entirely," he muttered to himself. He could hear the telephone ringing inside the house and looked up shaking his head.

Now the gossip will begin, he thought.

2

The family man

Peter was a perfect picture of confidence and success. He was married with three children and co-owned a chain of four restaurants with his wife, Sally. He was fifty-five and his wife three years younger.

They had been in business for some twenty-five years and made a good living from it. They had been together since their school days and had married young; he had been twenty and Sally eighteen, and pregnant with their first child, Susan. It was another ten years before the other two children came along but David was now fifteen and Henry thirteen.

Susan had graduated from university and for the past two years, she had been working in Guyana with the Caricom Secretariat. The two boys were still at secondary school. Peter was glad that Susan had decided to spread her wings and was hoping that she would decide to go even further afield to see the rest of the world.

One of the many things that he and Sally disagreed about was what the children should do after they had finished studying. She would have much preferred them to return home and find safe jobs as civil servants. However, he wanted his children to become citizens of the world and not become comfortable and insular, like the many others who had lived their lives on the small island.

Apart from that, there were very few eligible ambitious young men around. Peter had not been happy with the ones Susan has invited to the house. They were obsessed with their beauty, the latest designer clothes and the most recent electronic gadgets; they had very little interest in earning a living. In his restaurant, he had noticed that women were picking up the bill most of the time.

It appeared to him that today's young men were not prepared to work for a living, but rather that they preferred to rely on their 'other' illegal skills. Many seemed satisfied just sitting on the 'block' and watching the world go by. Each morning he would glance at them as he drove by, and sometimes he would even venture to greet them. However, from their expressions he got the impression that they were laughing at him. He could see their pity. He imagined them saying how stupid he was for getting out of his warm bed and going out to work.

However, at this precise moment, these young men were not at the forefront of Peter's mind. Neither did he have time to lament the Deacon's death, nor the circumstances surrounding his sudden passing. He had his own problems to consider. He knew he had behaved like an ass when he started his affair with Trina. Now he would have to bear the consequences, especially if his wife found out.

Trina had been the third applicant interviewed for the job of Personal Assistant. Peter had been glad that Sally had not turned up at the restaurant that day, because he was certain that she would not have selected Trina.

He was not even too sure, why he had chosen her, but as she entered his office, he had felt a stirring in his loins. It was the first time in a long time that he had felt such a strong sexual reaction. In fact, he could not recall the last time it happened with his wife. Trina's handshake had been warm and firm and she had allowed her hand to linger inside his after the shake. She looked confidently at him in the face.

Trina was twenty, rough and ready and had the hugest breasts that he had ever seen; they looked like two ripe melons ready to be plucked and sucked. She carried them well, with her height of approximately five feet eight inches and a weight of about one hundred and eighty pounds. When she walked, she strutted like a peacock. She wore the latest auburn shoulder-length weave, which constantly swung from side to side as she shook her head.

The interview itself had been very strange. Trina totally disarmed him with her business acumen and charm. He pondered over whether he should employ her, but she was definitely the best person that he had interviewed: she had the personality and the qualifications, but he did worry about whether he would be able to resist her. The interview had also been very flirtatious. Many women had thrown themselves at him over the years, including his friend Wendy. However, this time, he felt like he had had when he first met his wife. Therefore he wondered if he would succumb to Trina's advances.

Peter reckoned that Sally would need to take part of the blame for what had happened. He would not have felt the strong urge to go after Trina if Sally had been performing her wifely duties. For some years now, there had hardly been any intimacy between them. Sex had gone from several times a night to once a week, to once a month because Sally was too busy or too tired. Nowadays, it only took place on special occasions, Christmas and birthdays. She was either too busy dealing with church affairs or helping the Deacon.

He had intended to discuss this with Sally, but had not worked out how to broach the subject. He reflected on how far apart their relationship had grown since the Deacon had arrived in town.

Peter had tried very hard to conceal his relationship from Sally and anyone associated with his family and so far, it had worked. He was not too sure, however, how much longer the relationship could remain a secret. Wendy had seen them entering a hotel together and had threatened to expose him. She had followed and watched as they checked in.

The next day she turned up at his restaurant. She began by teasing him about his makeover and then Trina entered the restaurant to let him about a telephone call. Up to that point, Wendy didn't know that the person she had seen him with at the hotel had worked for him.

Wendy turned to watch Trina. As usual, Trina was leading with her boobs as she sauntered her way back into the office. Her head was erect, shoulders were back, and her arms swung loosely back and forth, and her hips swivelled from side-to-side. Wendy turned back to Peter. He jumped to his feet.

"Sorry," he said as he walked away from her towards his office.

The words Wendy had wanted to say didn't come out. She sat with her mouth open. She had originally come to see him to explain to him how disappointed she had been that he had preferred some 'girl' who looked and dressed as if she was going to bed and not necessarily to rest.

Wendy was furious and embarrassed. She got up abruptly and hurried out of the restaurant without a backward look.

3

The friend

Wendy telephoned Peter a week later to inform him of what she intended to do unless he visited her at her apartment so that they could talk.

Three weeks had passed since that call and his subsequent visit. Peter was still pondering what to do. He had a lot to lose if she followed through with the plan to disclose him to his wife.

Wendy was behaving as if she was a woman scorned. Perhaps she was. She was twenty-eight years old and worked in the lawyers' office next to his restaurant. She would come in from time-to-time to order her lunch or snack in the evenings before leaving for home.

Peter had always admired the way she dressed and her sense of correctness.

She would make someone a good wife someday, he used to think.

They became friends and sometimes he would sit with her as she ate her meal. One evening after she had stopped by to get some dinner to take home it began to rain heavily. When he was ready to leave, he offered her a lift home. During their many conversations, he had learnt that she lived in the same direction as him. She gratefully accepted. Taking her home each day after work became a habit thereafter whenever he worked late in the evenings.

One evening as he was about to drive away after dropping her off, she asked if he wanted to come in and have a drink of tea.

Peter was reluctant at first, because he liked to get home and spend time with Sally and the boys. However today, Sally had choir practice at the church, David had football practice and Henry had piano lessons. Additionally, since Sally would have already left home, he would not have to explain to her why he had arrived home later than usual. Therefore, he accepted.

Wendy lived on the ground floor of a building that contained four apartments. She unlocked the large mahogany door, walked into the room and held the door open for Peter. He stood in the doorway and surveyed the room. The front door opened into a large sitting room, dining room and kitchen combined.

Every piece of furniture in the room was white. Peter assumed it was an attempt to make the room look larger. Even the walls, the cupboards, the dining table, chairs, and the settee were white. The white furniture contrasted with lime-coloured floral curtains at the only bay window on one side of the wall, in the sitting room area. Underneath this window, a dining table and four chairs were neatly situated. There was a large framed oil painting on the wall on one side of the window. A tall mirror about three feet wide and eight feet high was on the opposite side. The kitchen was separated from the living room by a counter, which was about waist high.

"Welcome, to my home," she said smiling proudly, noting his observations.

She dropped her handbag and the food she had bought on the kitchen counter, and walked into the small kitchenette and lit the stove.

"Please take a seat."

Peter didn't sit right away, but continued to inspect the apartment. He could hear the tap running as she filled the kettle with water for the tea. He looked around when he heard the 'tick tick' of the stove been lit. It had been a long time since he had found himself in a house with a female, other than his wife, sister, mother, or daughter and he began to feel very ill at ease.

She must have sensed his anxiety because she continued to speak while she prepared the tea.

"I don't bite, and I promise I will not try to rape you, either." She looked in his direction and laughed awkwardly.

"At least...," she paused and winked at him. "...not today."

He smiled back and shook his head.

"I didn't think you would," he replied nervously, rubbing his hands together.

He put his car keys into the front pocket of his trousers. He pulled out one of the dining chairs and sat down.

She glanced at him and continued teasingly, "...But you never know, you might enjoy it."

He laughed again nervously.

The kettle whistled, and she busied herself making tea.

"Sugar, milk?" She asked without turning to face him.

"Both." He responded.

He continued to look around the room. There was a three-tiered bookshelf in one corner of the room and a magazine rack in front of it displaying some of the latest Oprah Winfrey magazines. One cover grabbed his attention. It said *"Finding and keeping the love of your life."*

"Can I look at one of your magazines?" He asked.

"Sure," she replied.

He got up and selected the magazine from the rack.

"Do you mind pouring your own tea?"

She walked over and placed a tray containing a teapot, a cup, sachets of sugar and a container with milk onto the table.

"I'm only good at making tea for myself. I think I used to make it badly deliberately as I didn't want to pour my mother's in the evenings when we watched TV."

"Really?" he responded and raised his brows.

Peter took the lid off the pot to make sure that the tea had drawn enough before he made his tea. She sat opposite and watched as he poured the tea, milk and sugar into the cup, and began stirring the contents with the spoon.

"I see that you've been well trained," she announced, nodding her head in approval. "I hope one of these days you can make tea for me since you seem to be so good at it."

"Thank you. Don't forget I run restaurants."

He shook the teapot.

"There's enough for two. Do you want me to make you a cup?"

"Nah, it's too early. I usually have a cup just before I go to bed," she said alluringly, "perhaps...if you're still here."

They looked at each other and laughed loudly and nervously.

Fifteen minutes later the atmosphere between Peter and Wendy was much more relaxed. Peter was on his second cup: he sipped his tea whilst browsing the magazine and Wendy continued to eat her dinner. He was not looking at anything in particular; he just wanted something to do with his hands.

"You have a nice place."

"Yes, but small. Thank you."

She looked around the room.

"I have had to be clever with the decorating to disguise the size."

"Yes, I noticed."

Peter continued to flip the pages of the magazine. She got up and began clearing the table. He took this as an indication that he should leave, so he closed the magazine and got up.

"Well, thank you for the tea," he said, and pushed his chair under the table.

She smiled, "And, thanks for keeping me company while I ate. It's been a long time since anyone has done that – I'm grateful."

She looked down at the table at the magazine that he had been reading.

"Oh! There's an article in there I would like you to read and maybe we can discuss it the next time we chat?"

She turned to the page and passed it over open at a page entitled, *"Love potion No 2009"*.

Peter looked at the title and read the first few sentences which seemed to be discussing "dating, marrying and chemistry and people who remarry the same person".

"I'm sorry, I don't get much time to read," Peter said, trying to give the magazine back.

"Please, please humour me."

Peter had enjoyed their chat. He found himself saying as he left. "We must do this again."

"Sure," she replied invitingly.

From then on, they began to meet regularly at her apartment. He would drink cups of tea and they would simply chat. They touched on every subject: politics, relationships, children, religion and their work. Peter found out that Wendy had been in several relationships, but none of them had worked out. She had been unfortunate as many men wanted children but not the associated commitment of raising them in a two-parent household. Peter had to admit that this wasn't unusual, but he wondered if it had not always been so.

Earlier in her life, she had wanted children, but not anymore. Now she wanted someone for a good time; someone who would leave at the end of the night, as she wished to live alone. She was wary of the type of men who you would invite to stay one night. Before you knew it their clothes would be all over the house; their friends would be calling them on your phone; their car would be permanently parked outside your house and neither would remember how this happened.

Wendy was easy to talk to and politically astute. She had studied law when she was younger, but had to give it up because of family difficulties. She had just applied to finish the course. She had even considered running for Parliament.

One evening after Peter had finished his tea, Wendy brought out a bottle of wine and two glasses from the fridge.

"Would you have a glass of wine with me? Tomorrow is my birthday."

She smiled, showing perfectly white teeth. She didn't wait for an answer, but instead popped the cork and poured the wine. Peter raised his hand to stop her, but he was already too late. He had never been good drinking anything alcoholic. Even the smell of alcohol made him dizzy. His friends always teased him about this. He had only been drunk once in his life and had almost killed his sister in a car accident as a consequence. He had therefore promised himself that he would never drink alcohol again, especially if he was driving. Moreover, he didn't want to arrive home with the smell on his breath. He would have no excuse for Sally because she knew that he never drank.

Wendy raised her glass.

"Well?" she queried looking at his filled glass still on the table. He wanted to explain but as he looked at her, he saw the disappointment in her eyes. She looked crestfallen.

Hell, he thought, *just this once*. He stood up, picked up the glass and raised it to touch hers.

"Happy birthday, for tomorrow."

Peter finished the wine in one gulp and returned the glass to the table. She slowly sipped hers watching him over the rim.

"Have another, please," she insisted, trying to pour him more wine. He covered the top with his hand.

"No." he replied firmly whilst looking at his watch. "I really must go."

He picked up his car keys and began to walk towards the door. Wendy also moved to stand between him and the door.

"So, what are going to give me for my birthday?" she asked, her arms outstretched.

"How about a hug?"

By now she was standing very close to Peter, and he could smell her perfume.

She smells good, he thought. *But this is not for me*. "What the hell." He said aloud. He hugged her.

"Mmmm," she groaned.

Wendy pushed her body against Peter's. He didn't know much about perfume, but she smelt of sunflowers and cocoa butter. That smell and the wine overwhelmed him and he grew nauseous.

Peter could feel her breasts hard against his chest. She was pressing herself against him and rubbing her groin against his. Her arms were vice-like – she began to groan and rotate her hips.

"This feels so good," she said. She looked up into his face.

"Make love to me tonight," she whispered in his ear, "it's my birthday, let it be my gift from you," she begged, pressing her body full length against his, and kissing him on his left ear. "No one has to know."

She bit him gently on his left lobe, and then stuck her tongue inside his ear.

He tried to extricate himself, but the more he tried, the tighter her grip became.

"Please, please, he implored, as he struggled to loosen her grip. "I need to get home."

He was embarrassed, and didn't know what to say in reply to her suggestion.

"I, I, love my wife, I don't think I can."

He held onto her shoulders with both hands and pushed her away.

"I like you very much as a friend, and if we do this it would change our relationship forever. I, I cannot be unfaithful to my wife."

"Peter," she pleaded looking at him with tears welling up in her eyes. "I have loved you, from the first moment we met. I can't hold back anymore; I really need you tonight. I dream about you every night. You, you, making passionate love to me."

She grabbed his hand and attempted to drag him into her bedroom.

Peter pulled away, again holding her at arms length.

"No, I can't do it," he said resolutely.

He held his head. It was spinning. The wine and her perfume were making him nauseous. He worried that he would vomit.

Please, I have protection; you don't have to wor..."

Peter interrupted.

"Wendy, no," he said firmly, "you're very beautiful, very sexy, but I can't do it. I just can't."

Tears were falling down her face. He released her and walked swiftly towards the door. He looked back at her from the step. "I'm sorry," he whispered. "I just ca..."

She was standing at the door staring at him. He could see that she was fuming. She didn't wait to hear the end of his sentence, and slammed the door.

He sighed, sat back in the car and turned the engine on.

What just happened? he asked himself.

He really liked her, but not enough to have a sexual relationship with her. Besides he loved his wife very much. Even though he had broken his vows twice, he had promised himself that he would never do so again as the risks were too great.

It had been over two years since Peter had rejected Wendy's advances. After that evening, when she had tried to get him to kiss her, she had avoided him like the plague. Subsequently they had hardly seen or spoken to each other: She had bought herself a car, so there was no longer a need for him to offer her lifts. She still came in for lunch, but apart from the salutary "Good morning" or Good afternoon" they hardly spoke.

Peter feared that their relationship would never return to where it had been. Their happy-go-lucky friendship had gone forever. He deeply regretted this, as, for the first time in his life, he thought that he had a female friend with no strings attached.

Now, however, he had a big problem. As he had rejected Wendy's advances, she was now going to make him pay. She had told him this three days ago. He had to find a way to stop her going to Sally. Giving up Trina was not an option. Just the mere mention of her name would make his body react; his hands began to sweat and his loins tingle. He needed Trina in his life. He touched his crotch. A part of him needed her in the same way that he needed his wife.

He could never let anyone else find out about the affair, especially his wife. He had to find a solution and presently he had no idea what to do. Wendy wanted him and he knew that there was only one way to stop her from exposing his relationship with Tricia.

The sudden death of the Deacon, therefore, was not the foremost thing on Peter's mind that morning. He had feared that when Sally had shouted his name earlier, it was to open a "conversation" about his affair. However, on reflection she would not handle it that way; she was too dignified to discuss such matters so openly.

.

4

Age is a number

Peter hummed the calypso, *Age is just a number* by the famous calypsonian Sparrow, as he checked himself out in the mirror.

He was pleased with the result: he was rejuvenated. He could not recall the last time he had felt so good about his appearance. He felt like a teenager. Whistling loudly he approached his parked car. He felt as if all the women he passed on this short walk were staring approvingly. One young woman had actually whistled as she walked by. He could not stop himself gazing at his reflection in the car. His barber had done a very good job on his face and hair.

He liked his new look; not one grey hair was showing in his beard. He now just had to remember not to frown too often so as to avoid 'banks' forming on his forehead. He mused on the irony of him now spending time each morning practising how to raise his eyebrows without causing lines to form, when as a child he and his sisters were fascinated with their grandfather's 'banks'. They would beg the old man constantly to raise his eyebrows just so they could feel the folds that formed on his forehead.

Peter had begun this remodelling of himself to get Trina's attention. He had to convince her that he was the man for her. He had researched and rehearsed all the things that he would say. He had tried to anticipate all her questions and objections and knew all the possible answers that would make her believe that a relationship with him was the best thing for her.

If she were to say that, he was old enough to be her father, he would refer to all the famous people who had successful relationships in spite of the age differences. These included Bob Marley's mother who had had a relationship with a man who was much older than herself and Nelson and Winnie Mandela. Winnie had waited patiently for twenty years until Nelson was released from prison.

He would explain that if she didn't love him now that they would grow to love each other. He would speak about the ratio of woman to men in the world and her chances of finding a man of her own. He would persuade her that it would be better to share with someone else since the chances of finding a man was limited because of this disparity.

"Let's spread the love," he would tell her. He would admonish her by saying, "No one should tell you who to be with. That is your decision. However, I want you so badly and you should not think about our ages. Age should not matter, as long as we want to be together. We can do things together."

He would promise her those things that she couldn't afford. "Yes," he told himself as he prepared himself to speak to her, "they like things, especially if they cannot find the money to buy them for themselves." "Have you ever been on a cruise?" he would ask her. "We would take one together." He was certain that she would not know what a real cruise was, so he would say to her, "No, not like the Jolly Roger, that goes along the coast. No, not like that, we can do a Caribbean cruise at least once a year, if that's what you want."

However, he didn't need to go through the different speeches he had practiced and spoken aloud in front of the mirror and in his mind, because Trina made the first move.

She had walked into his office crying and explaining that her mother had been in a fight with another woman and that she had been taken to hospital with a stab wound. He offered her a lift there and afterwards, to take her home if she wished. Thankfully it turned out to be just a flesh wound and that Trina's mother had been treated and discharged before Trina even got to the hospital.

Therefore, Trina decided that she would prefer to return to the office and finish her work. At five o'clock that evening, she walked into Peter's office and asked if he could give her a lift to the gym instead. He agreed. When they arrived there, she asked if he wanted to come in and do some exercise. She touched his arm, squeezing it gently. She allowed her hand to linger on his arm as she said, with a sly smile, "I think you could do with some work here."

She's flirting with me. He thought, but aloud he said.

"Not today, maybe another time; besides I have no gym clothes."

"OK," she agreed.

She opened the car door to get out, but before getting out, she said, "Maybe we can shop for some clothes for you," she paused, "tomorrow?"

She showed the gym card to him. "I only have this for another week, so maybe we can use it tomorrow."

She paused again. "You can be my guest, right?"

She waited for him to reply. He was nodding, so she took that to mean assent.

"Bye," she said and closed the car door noisily. "See you tomorrow."

She walked away from the car before he could gather his thoughts. He was not too sure, what he had just agreed to. He wanted to call her back to question her, but she had already walked into the gym.

Peter knew that Trina was right. He needed to keep looking young and fit, especially now that he had decided he wanted a younger lover. Joining a gym had been on his mind for some time. He had noticed of late that the skin on his upper arms and thighs was becoming loose. Now that Trina had also pointed it out, he knew that he must do something about it. However, before doing so, he would need to have a good reason for his wife.

The next day Trina phoned to say that she was going to be late as she needed to collect something. When she arrived at work, she walked into Peter's office and dropped a shopping bag on his desk; the contents scattered all over the place.

"You owe me," she announced and began taking out and unwrapping various parcels. She handed him the receipts.

"Should I take it from petty cash?"

He looked at the contents with a puzzled expression on his face, but said nothing. He began to scrutinise the items: a pair of sneakers, a tracksuit, and two pairs of socks.

Trina was standing over him, hands on her hips, and tapping her foot on the floor. Peter could not look at her, for fear of giving himself away.

How did things move so fast? He thought. *I was supposed to be pursuing her.*

"Well," she continued adamantly.

Yeah, yeah," he finally replied. "Take it from petty cash. I'll return it later this afternoon when I go to the bank. Thank you." He looked at her and smiled.

"You should try them on though." She began to walk out of the room and looking back at him said, "Because I guessed your size."

She smiled back whilst closing his door quietly.

5

Snared

Sally had taken the other changes, his shaved head, dyed beard and pierced ears in good heart. She and the children had laughed about it and she had even helped with his beard when it needed re-dyeing. His daughter had jokingly asked:

"When are you going to get the sports car, Dad?"

However, joining a gym was something that both he and Sally had frowned upon in the past. They used to tell each other that they would grow old 'gracefully' together. He recalled how he and Sally used to laugh at Nigel their neighbour when he began to dye his hair, bought a sports car, and began to wear the latest fashion, including piercing his ears and inserting two gold earrings.

Nigel was sixty at the time and had just lost his wife. Within a year, he had married a woman, who was twenty years his junior. He remembered Nigel's daughter, Jennifer, visiting Peter and Sally and begging them to speak to her father, as he was making a fool of himself. They declined, as it was none of their business.

Ultimately, Nigel sold his house and moved to another part of the island where, according to the rumours, he and his new bride were living happily with their two young children. The difference between him and Nigel was that he would not be looking to marry, because he had no intention of leaving his wife for anyone. The last thing he wanted to do was to break up his marriage. He, therefore, didn't want to arouse Sally's suspicions, so anything else he did, such as join a gym, would have to be carefully planned. He would have to think of a good reason to join without first discussing with her. At the same time, he knew that if he wished to keep Trina interested he had to be fit and look good.

Peter accompanied Trina to the gym as her guest the next day; he paid full membership for her that day. He didn't enrol himself, instead, they decided that he would join her from time-to-time, paying for his individual visits. It would be more costly for him, but he felt it would be safer.

He was dressed in the gym outfit that Trina had bought. She whistled her approval when she saw him told him how good he looked. She showed him how to use the different pieces of equipment and helped him with his warm-up and exercise routine.

The Beautiful Body Gym was the place where Peter and Trina first made love. Peter remembered vividly what happened on his second visit to the gym as Trina's guest. It was not only the first they made love; but it was also the first time he had ever had a sauna.

The sauna had been recently installed and after their training Trina suggested that they should try it out. They entered the room and she immediately took the towel away from around her body and stood before him naked. She pulled his towel away too and embraced him.

He could not resist her magnetism as she began kissing him gently, on the lips, the nose and his eyes. She stuck her tongue into his ear. The sensation was magical and he giggled like a baby.

"Ssssshhhhh," she whispered and moved to the other ear. Initially he tried to resist and kept looking at the glass pane in the door. However, Trina had locked the door and had placed a face cloth over the glass. He gave in, relaxed his body and let her take charge.

He had never done anything as outrageous as he did in that sauna. He was certain that others could hear them groaning and moaning. She was very persuasive, very inventive, showing him different positions, different angles that she wanted him to try and he obliged. Trina had snared him. He knew that there was no turning back.

He continued to visit the gym as her guest once a week. To stop Sally becoming suspicious of his toned body, he took to jogging three evenings a week after work. Initially, he invited her to join him but she refused, saying that she was too busy 'saving souls for the Lord'. Sometimes, one or other of his sons would join him.

Trina persuaded him to buy new clothes to match his new look. They went shopping together and she helped him pick out a few 'things'. He brought them home and explained to his wife that his sister, who lived in the States, had sent them to him. He knew this was safe as Sally would never contact his sister as they had never got on.

Peter met many of Trina's friends. He was surprised at how many were actively looking for older men. Young men, they said, didn't know how to treat a woman. Peter had to agree. He had noticed this problem when his daughter brought men home from time to time.

"They don't work, and don't really want to work." Trina's friends would say.

From the conversations he had with Trina and from what he overheard when she was speaking with friends, it appeared that young women these days could be divided into three categories: those who choose to live alone or with female partners; those who were financially independent and only wanted men or 'boys' to have a child and then dump them; or those, who wanted a man who could support them and maybe even buy them a car or an apartment. Each group would grab all that they could before moving on to their next 'victim'.

Peter surmised that love played little or no part in these relationships. He wondered which group Trina belonged to. So far, Trina had not asked for much, but he recalled her mother Maureen's interrogation when they had met.

Who were his family? His mother's family name? Where did they originate? Where were his businesses located?" She also asked if there were any vacancies at the other branches and seemed disappointed when he explained that the branches were all franchises so he didn't control how they were run, or whom they employed. Maureen then explained that she had another daughter who was looking for work and asked if he had a business friend who might be able to help.

"You know," she said waving her hand in the air and winking at him.

Yes, he knew exactly what she meant because Trina had explained some of her family history to him.

6

Inheritance

Trina came from a long line of woman who knew how to manipulate men to get what they needed to survive. Daley women had a reputation. They knew how to exaggerate their attractiveness and how to focus on displaying and flaunt their attributes and use this to get whatever they wanted. These women ensnared many men.

Trina's great grandmother, Janet Daley, grandmother, Sandra Daley and mother, Maureen, all relied on their manipulative skills to survive. It didn't matter whether the men were married, engaged, or single. They would track them down once there was the slightest possibility of getting something from them. Wives, mothers, and girlfriends were all wary of them. They would try their best to monitor their men's activities whenever they had to be in contact with these women. Yet the manipulation continued with Trina, and her sister, Tracy. The Daley women knew what they wanted and didn't hesitate to go out of their way to get it.

They were never actively referred to as prostitutes, because you would never find them walking the streets looking for men or favours. Nevertheless, they would use their womanly wiles to trap men with money or status. They would draw them into their web before seducing them in order to enrich themselves.

Trina was groomed by her mother, her aunts and older cousins. They, in turn, had been groomed by earlier generations. Generation to generation, they had successfully won hearts, money and property in pursuit of a better life.

Trina wanted Peter from the day that she had attended the interview. Her mother and older sister helped her prepare. They had advised her and made sure that she wore appropriate clothes and accessories that would display her well-proportioned body at its best. She saw how he had shuddered when she entered the room and knew immediately that he would be putty in her hands. She just had to select the right place and time to seduce him.

The first thing that she noticed about Peter was his eyes followed by the dimple in his chin. He reminded her of her only brother, whose eyes were huge and a beautiful hazel. She remembered as she was growing up wishing that she had eyes like her brother. He had inherited them from their grandmother together with the chin dimple. The eyes she could do nothing about, but she used to spend a lot of time, pushing her finger into her chin hoping that she would develop a dimple, just like her brother. Now here was someone with both those attributes.

She thought to herself as she looked at Peter. *Maybe our children will inherit them.*

Consequently, when Peter planned to seduce Trina she was way ahead of him. She had already discussed her seduction plans with her mother and had received full acknowledgement and consent.

Her mother had taught her how to be flirtatious, how to relax and smile, how to use her body language to give signals that she was a fun person and that she was someone who was comfortable and confident. She knew how to touch briefly and gently as she spoke. She had learned how to be assertive; how to hold hands should they be crossing the street; how to lead a man gently holding his arm towards a table in a restaurant. Her mother had instilled in her that touching in this way helped to break the "personal space" barrier. What she didn't learn from her mother she instead learnt from her Great, Aunt Susan, who spoke to her about the need to keep her hands warm, because to touch with a cold hand unconsciously makes a person judge you as frigid.

Trina remembered evenings when she and her sister sat in their tiny bedroom, listening to Grandmother Sandra talk to them about seduction and how it was synonymous with body warmth. She taught them the importance of caution; how to back off if there were negative or mixed signals. She demonstrated how they should place their hands on a man's body after they said hello and that the most effective move was to touch a man's thigh, whilst making eye contact and licking your lip. They would practise on each other in their Gran Aunt Susan's bedrooms.

They would dress in some of her underwear whilst she informed them that it was best not to wear any, but that if they did they should make sure that it was exposed and looked hot.

"Show your underwear, or better yet wear none," she advised.

She told them that they should either wear black bras with straps to peek out from underneath their tops or no bra so that their nipples would show through the top.

Trina recalled the many things that her mother, aunt and cousins explained. One of the main things her mother had taken pains to outline was that men were insecure: they didn't know what they really wanted and therefore might not make the first move. If a man failed to do so in a timely manner, then the decision should be made for him, because he would admire the boldness and confidence shown.

"Assume that he likes you and wants you," she would say. "Give him two positive options before you move in to close the deal. Say something like, 'Do you want us to have sex now, or later?' Then smile demurely, and begin to undress."

At this point, she would demonstrate the actions. "And, finally, when there's no negative option available to him, he will choose a positive course of action."

Their mother would tell them that the very house they lived in was built on their grandmother, Sandra's, hard work.

Trina and Tracey spent many nights sitting at the feet of their grandmother and mother listening to these stories learning what they had to do in order to survive. They knew that their grandmother had been deserted first by her father, and then by Thomas, Maureen's father.

7

Family ties - Sandra

Sandra Daley, Trina's grandmother, should have escaped the grooming. Perhaps if that had happened then Trina would have been a different person. However, Sandra, after living with her father, his new wife and her grandparents in the country for eight years, returned to her mother when her grandparents died and her father and his wife decided to migrate to Canada.

Sandra was five years old when her father took her to live with him. He had arrived at her mother Janet's house early one Saturday morning to take Sandra for a long weekend with him and found her asleep in the same bed as Janet and her new boyfriend.

Apparently, he became very annoyed, even though when he had his affair with Janet, he used to share the same bed with Janet and Sandra's brother, Benjamin, when he was about the same age as Sandra now was. The following weekend Trina's grandfather informed Janet that he wanted Sandra to live with him. Janet agreed because he threatened to no longer support Sandra if she didn't.

Sandra cried as she and her father walked away from her mother's house. Her mother, her two aunts, their children and her brother Benjamin, were standing in front of the house waving goodbye. Her father pried her away from her mother's leg and she wept because she didn't want to go; she didn't want to leave the family and friends that she had known all her life. She had spent weekends with her father, but she didn't want to live with him. She was going to miss her family, but more than ever, she would miss her best friend, Martha. The only consolation was that her father had promised her that during the long summer holidays she would return to the village.

Sandra loved her mother's village for many reasons. Her mother and her other relatives, lived close to the sea and she would spend a lot of time frolicking in and out of the water with the other girls and younger boys. Very few of them knew how to swim, however. Even though Sandra had begged her mother to let her learn, she had steadfastly refused.

When she had asked her mother why she had to go to live with her father, she had replied that it was because his wife could not have children. Yet, she had overheard her father and his wife speaking about "rescuing her from becoming a prostitute like the rest of the Daley clan". When she asked her mother what that statement meant; her she simply threw back her head and laughed saying that they were jealous. She explained emphatically that her father's wife didn't know how to please a man, and "we know how to please a man and can have any man that we want".

"Lots of women are jealous of us, dear. You'll find out when you get older."

"What do you mean, Ma?" she'd asked.

Her mother had laughed again and said, "Like I said, 'When, you're old enough you'll find out.'"

It was years later that Martha had explained to her what the word 'prostitute' meant. However, even after the explanation, she still didn't understand why that word was used to describe her family.

Country life was different from her life in the village. Her father and his wife managed her grandfather's farm. Her grandfather had had an accident years earlier and was unable to walk; her father paid two workers to help. Her father's wife did the office work and Sandra would work with her grandmother to help with the housework. When it was time to reap the vegetables, fruit and flowers that they grew, everyone had to help. Sandra grew to hate this time of year because there was so much work to do. When Sandra was with her mother she had no chores.

Furthermore, the school she now attended served the children from all the local farms and the school population never went beyond thirty students all of varying ages. She never saw the other students after school: some were driven to and from by their parents in trucks; some rode their bikes; others trekked home on foot. She would only see them on Sundays at church, or other special occasions, such as fairs, at harvest time or when the church's Mothers Union arranged special functions, which she would attend with her grandmother.

Sandra, therefore, spent a lot of time by herself or helping her grandmother around the house. In the evenings, she played board games with her grandfather as they listened to the radio.

"

8

Coveville

Sandra was extremely excited when at nine-years-old she was finally allowed to return to her mother for the summer. Her father had kept postponing her visit to Coveville, even though she had begged him to let her go back. He said that she needed to settle in the country.

She had been away for three years, but once she had learned to write properly, she began to write regularly to her mother and also to Martha. Martha would tell her about the changes that were taking place in the village since she had left. Every night, especially during the summer months, she dreamt about the village.

She was glad to be back in Coveville. Her brother took her on a tour of the main street with the new stalls and buildings that had now become a part of the beach. She loved spending time with her big brother who took her everywhere, even to the dockyard where he was to begin work shortly. People would stop him and ask who she was. Sometimes he would say and sometimes he would not. As they walked along the main road, he advised her whom she should speak to and whom she should ignore. Whilst she walked, she thought that Martha was right; the village was very different from the one she had left.

Apart from the new stalls, there were new people and a new friend, Thomas, whom Martha introduced to her earlier that summer. Thomas was thirteen-years-old and his family had just arrived in town. They lived on the outskirts of the village where all the rich people lived. He attended a private school in the city, but in the evenings, he could be found on the pier fishing, with the other village boys.

Martha no longer lived in the village, but instead stayed with her grandmother in the city and like Sandra, would visit the village during the summer. Nowadays, however, she worked with her father on his fishing stall and had very little time to spend with Sandra. Some days Sandra would visit her at the stall and watch her as she worked. Sometimes Thomas would join her. They always had to disappear when Martha's father arrived. All he needed to do was to clear his throat and both Sandra and Thomas would leave.

Some things in the village remained the same. There were activities day and night, especially at the weekend. Coveville was the second largest village in the country and was known for its conch soup, lobster tails and fried fish, in particular, jacks. It was also the only port outside of the city. This was where the tourist cruise ships, private sailing vessels, ships and vessels landing people, ships delivering goods and parcels and barrels for the families with relatives abroad docked.

The beach was a perfect semi-circle in the centre of which stood a pier jutting out about three hundred feet into the water. This is where vessels that were able to dock would dock; the larger ones had to dock further out and ferry their passengers and merchandise in smaller boats.

Sandra's mother's house was in a cluster of similar homes built along a ridge overlooking the local beach. Her family has always lived in Coveville.

On a clear day, the full length of the six-hundred-feet-or-so beach was visible from the ridge. You could sit and gaze at the ebb and flow of the water extending from touching the toes of early-morning sea bathers to the horizon where ships appeared to fall of the edge of the world as they disappeared from sight. At one end of this semi-circle, was a huge rock, extending about two hundred feet into the sea. It stood about one hundred feet high.

Sandra would watch as the early morning deep blue water, turned into a brilliant turquoise as the midday sun shone majestically upon it, the blue sky reflected within. She would spend her early mornings watching the older men as they fished from this rock with their long rods made of bamboo. Other men were in the water throwing nets this way and that, while their small fishing boat seemed to follow them around in the water. Mostly these men would be fishing for bait, which they would use later when they took their fishing boats out to sea.

Later in the day, especially at weekends or during the long summer days, a new set of inhabitants would take over the rock. These would be the younger men and boys including her brother, Benjamin. They would dive off the rock into the water, yelling and screaming with excitement as they went. They would compete to see who could stay in the air the longest, who could stay under the water the longest, who could go deepest, or who took the shortest time to return to the shore after the dive.

Sandra loved to watch the boys in mid-air as they would be spin their legs as if riding bicycles, or as if they were trying to take off like a bird heading towards to horizon.

Then there were the "permanent" inhabitants of the rock and the surrounding shore and water. These were different types of birds, crabs and turtles, which spent their days and nights in and out of the water, or amongst the rocks. Big birds skimmed the water's surface. Little birds ran around in the surf, chasing the waves, eating small creatures in the sand, like the little crabs and crustaceans.

Her brother told her about the female turtles that crawled out on the beaches at night to dig nests and lay eggs before making their way back into the water. Weeks later, the hatchlings would emerge and they too, would head to sea. The men of the village would wait for the turtles as they made their way back into the water and capture them. There was always great excitement during this period, because, the older children would sneak out at night to watch them.

Off in the distance, looking over from the ridge, there seemed to be buildings on the water's edge. However, that was not so, as an asphalt road, the main artery to other parts of the country separated the long beach from the buildings.

These buildings were mostly made from galvanized iron, though some were made from wood and stone or cement blocks, with coconut or straw for the roof. The only completely stone building was a church with a wooden roof and a cross on its steeple. It was the tallest building in the village.

Vendors, selling fish, coconut water, sugarcane juice, ground provisions and other everyday groceries were housed in the other buildings. There were several rum shops and a dance hall. There was also a boat builders shed. Next to this shed were boats in various stages of completion or repair. She loved to watch boat-builders as they worked.

Today Sandra had arranged to meet Thomas at Martha's father stall. They were sitting on a bench outside the stall awaiting Martha's arrival, when they heard the sound of the conch shell. It echoed throughout the village, announcing that fish was on sale. They rushed like everyone else towards the sound.

They spied a lone fishing boat and it was already surrounded with people. It seemed as if all the women of the village had descended upon it. Even before the boat had landed on the beach, the crowd was fighting to get to the front of the queue.

Sandra and Thomas knew from experience that pandemonium would ensue as each woman asserted her right to be served first, or to get the best cut, or the largest serving. The haggling invariably ended with the police having to intervene as the women would inevitably end up fighting each other, the fisherman, or even their own boyfriends or husbands who would appear on the scene. Today, however, they had surrounded the wrong fishing boat.

The sound of the conch was heard again. This time, from about one hundred yards further up the cove. Everyone including Sandra and Thomas began to run towards the boat. Those who had gathered for fish began running in the direction of the sound of the conch shell, which had continued to call.

Sandra could see her Aunt Marva and Donna Phipps running head to head in front of everyone else. Though they arrived at the boat first it didn't take long before the boat became surrounded. Everyone pressed forward so that they could get served first. Some of the crowd were calling the names of the three fishermen and shouting their orders.

Sandra and Thomas have perched themselves on an upside boat so that they had a better view of what was happening. Sandra could see her Aunt and Donna shoving each other to get served first.

"Don't push me, you." Aunt Marva shouted angrily.

"You push me first," was the reply from Donna Phipps. She pushed her forefinger into her Aunt's face as she spoke crossly."I got here first."

"Move your stinking finger out of my face," was her Aunt's replied even more irate. She slapped the hand away from her face.

"You hit me. You hit me," Donna Phipps screamed at her.

Then the fight began. As a potential witness it would have been difficult for anyone who was present to say which of the two women actually started the fight.

Fish and fists flew everywhere. The women not caught up with the fight held out their skirts to catch fish flying about their heads whilst they dodged and weaved in an attempt to escape the fists.

In the meantime, her Aunt and Donna were rolling around on the muddy ground amongst the majority of the fallen fish. Fists were flying here, there and everywhere. Both women were cursing. Sandra was familiar with some of the words but others she made a mental note of to ask Martha about later.

One minute her Aunt was on top and the next minute Donna was on top. The crowd was gradually growing larger. There was great hilarity amongst them as they watched what was happening in front of them. Some of the women had gathered so much fish that they were pushing what they could not hold in their skirts into their brassieres and panties.

Sandra's Aunt was now on top of Donna with her knees in her belly whilst she punched her in the face. Donna's head was rocking from side to side. Both women were down to their undies and Marva's breasts had fallen out of her brassiere into Donna's face and threatened to smother her.

Suddenly Marva was pulled off Donna by a burly police officer, who literally dropped her on her buttocks. She fell with a 'thud'. Donna was helped to her feet. Clothes were brought to both women so they could cover themselves. They continued to curse and threaten each other, until the police officer warned that if they didn't stop, he would arrest them for breaching the peace and any other charges, which he could find in the book. Things quietened quickly once the police arrived.

After the infamous 'fish woman fight' as the incident later became known, Sandra understood more clearly what she had missed in the past three years she was not allowed to visit Coveville.

Donna and Marva were made to repay the fishermen for all the fish they had lost that day. They were also banned from approaching any fishing boat for the following two years.

Sandra was glad that she was able to visit once again and to see her mother, brother and other relatives. Moreover she was ecstatic that she was able to bond with Martha and her new friend Thomas. In particular, she had missed the area everyone who lived there referred to as the strip.

At night, the street that ran between the beach and the street, the 'Strip', morphed into a bubbling, lantern-lit hive of activity, with a carnival atmosphere. This was especially true of Friday and Saturday nights, when people from all around the country and tourists would visit. At night other people took over. The drunks, the prostitutes, the drug pushers and users, the stray dogs, cats, sheep and goats of the village and a bible-totting preacher who would stand outside his church beseeching everyone who passed to enter the church to seek salvation, instead of visiting the dens of 'iniquity'.

The 'Strip' would become dense with food sellers and their customers. The aroma from their stalls was intoxicating. Fish, pork, mutton, could be bought grilled, fried or roasted. It would be served on a delicate bed of rice, or other types of ground provisions. "

You could also find roasted sweet potatoes and corn. Fish would be the most popular protein of the night and the sellers would call, "Fish! Fish! Come and get your fried fish!" The food that was consumed would be washed down with coconut water, or rum – straight, iced, or watered, or another beverage of choice.

Every summer for the next three years Sandra came 'home' to Coveville and even though things changed during those years, the basic exciting things that made the village and the Strip what it is and what everyone who lived there and visited there expected remain constant. Her friendship with Martha and Thomas also blossomed during those years.

9

Love and hate

Sandra was sitting on a huge stone on the ridge watching the activities on the beach. She twelve years old and spending another summer in Coleville. She had arrived the evening before. She told her mother that she wanted to go to bed immediately so that she could be up early to meet with her friends Martha and Thomas.

From the previous year, she had planned with Thomas that they would try and spend as much time together as possible. They had kept in touch during the year. They had planned to meet on the ridge. She hoped he would turn up soon before her cousins did. She had not yet seen them but they would know that now she had arrived.

She heard someone shout her name. She looked in her direction of the voice and saw Annie running towards her. She was waving frantically.

"Saaaaaaaaaaaaandra, Saaaaaaaaaaaaaandra, Saaaaaaaaaandra,"

Annie continued to shout even though Sandra had waved at her to acknowledge that she had both heard and seen her.

She rushed up to Sandra and hugged her roughly by the shoulders. She nuzzled her chin into Sandra's shoulder blade. Sandra felt her breath on her ear. It tickled her. She shifted her position. Annie smelt of carbolic soap. Sandra wondered if she had used that to brush her teeth.

"Come; come let's go to our house, Millie want to see you." Annie continued not giving Sandra time to say anything to greet her. She grabbed at her hand and began to pull her off the rock. "Let's surprise her. She's not even up yet."

No, no, Sandra thought.

That was the last thing she wanted. She no longer wanted to play with her cousins. The last time she was with them in their mother's house, Mildred, lay down on the bed and asked Annie to lie on top of her. They began playing with her titties and kissing each other on the mouth. Sandra remembered vividly that Mildred had demonstrated what she wanted Sandra to do with Annie. Sandra had walked out of the house and left them playing 'their' game. Since then, she had stayed away from them, unless other family members were around.

"Its good to see you Annie," Sandra replied finally. "I'm waiting for Thomas. He promised he would meet me hear, this morning."

Annie looked very disappointed.

"But, but. You can see him from the house. You, you don't have to wait here. Please come," she pleaded.

She pulled at her hand again.

Sandra looked down the path once more. There was no sign of Thomas. He was already late.

"Ok," she said. "I'll come. But only for half an hour and then I'm going into to find Martha."

She was only in the house ten minutes when she heard Martha shouting her name. She had half an hour before she had to open her father's stall. They walked to the pier where they met Thomas fishing.

"Hi you two," Thomas said looking up from his line.

"Hi," Martha replied and sat down next to him. Sandra sat next to Martha. The water was clear and they could see fish circling the bait on Thomas's line. However, none of them was biting.

"Sorry about not meeting you as promised Sandra, but since Martha was coming I thought that I would wait here for you too."

"That's ok," Sandra replied.

She didn't want him to know that she was disappointed that he didn't meet her. She was looking forward to seeing him even more so than Martha.

"This is such a waste of time today," he said irritated. "I would usually have caught something by now."

Thomas tied his line onto the pier and they walked to the end of the pier discussing the picnic planned for a few days later. Suddenly, Sandra heard her name shouted. They looked around and saw Benjamin walking hurriedly towards them.

He walked up to Thomas pointing his finger in his face and shouting.

"What are you doing with them? You!"

He pushed Thomas hard in the chest, forcing him to take a step back. Thomas said and didn'thing. He looked at the girls and then down at his feet.

"Leave him alone," Martha said angrily, looking at Benjamin defiantly. "You're such a bully."

She poked Benjamin on the arm.

"One of these days, I'll show how much of a bully I really am," he threatened.

They looked at each other in silence for a moment.

Benjamin nodded his head, pulled Sandra by the arm and began dragging her behind him off the pier. Sandra didn't resist but followed obediently.

"Just keep away from my sister," he warned looking back at Thomas.

He walked Sandra towards the boatyard. Martha didn't follow them. She stood next to Thomas laughing loudly. She shouted after them.

"See you later, Sandra."

Sandra didn't reply. She was annoyed with her brother. He was constantly telling her what to do. It seemed that every time he saw her speaking to a boy, he intervened.

"What's wrong with you?" She asked him. "They're my friends."

"Keep away from him, I warn you," he replied angrily.

'But..., but...," she began to argue.

"Oh, shut up," Benjamin interrupted.

He bent down so that he could look into her face.

"I said to stay fucking away from him, you understand," he screamed.

His eyes were red and were glaring at her. She was scared and at that moment, she hated him. She remembered how he had escorted her around when she first returned that first summer. Benjamin had changed. He was always angry. He was not the loving brother from previous years. Instead he constantly shouted or hit her. That first summer he had shown her the shed where he worked as an apprentice, even though he knew he could get into trouble. There was a large sign on the huge wooden gate in front of the shed that stated, 'No Trespassing, Workers only'. She begged him to take her inside. He did, but made her promise that she would not tell their mother.

"Don't touch anything," he had warned, as she walked around the large shed looking at the boats at their different stages of completion, some high in the air and others on the ground. The equipment used by the men was neatly placed on large tables or hanging on the walls of the shed.

Today, Benjamin was a stranger to her. Benjamin had built a reputation around town as a bully. He had taken up bodybuilding and would get into fights at weekends. The police were frequently coming to the house because he had beaten up someone on the 'Strip'. His mother would scream profanity at the police as they took Benjamin away. They always warned her that she would be arrested too, but that never happened. Benjamin had also started spending a lot of time, when not at work, on the beach parading his well-oiled body to the tourists. He only seemed interested in clothes, combing his hair and putting on strong-smelling cologne that he had bought from the hairdresser's shop, drinking alcohol and beating up those who got in his way.

Two days later, however, Benjamin was the last person on Sandra's mind. She was excited, because she was going to a picnic on the beach with some of the other children, including Thomas and Martha. Everyone was expected to contribute food and drink. However, Sandra wouldn't have to bring anything because Martha and Thomas had promised to bring enough for the three of them. Thomas was going to bring his fishing rod to do some fishing and had said that any fish he caught was Sandra's.

All types of food were promised, including breadfruits and sweet potatoes which they planned to roast in an open fire; red herring and salt pork and, if they were lucky, they would also have fish to roast.

All the excitement dissolved into disenchantment for Sandra. Martha didn't show. Unfortunately, today was not Thomas's lucky day the fish weren't biting. Therefore, there was not enough food to go around, so today, instead of staying on the beach until late in the evening; Sandra had to return home to get the lunch that her mother had prepared for her.

As she entered her mother's small two-roomed house, she heard voices inside her mother's bedroom.

"Ma," she shouted.

The voices went quiet; the bedroom door opened and her brother Benjamin came out. He had only his trousers on. At sixteen-years-old, Benjamin looked much older. He already had the beginnings of a beard.

"What brought you back here?" he asked irately.

He was holding onto the door, but Sandra could see someone behind him.

"Who's that?" she asked enquiringly. She tiptoed so that she could see beyond his head.

"None of your business. Now shove off, before I slap you."

He raised his hand as if to hit her. Sandra winced and began to back away.

"But, but my lunch."

She pointed to the paper bag, which she knew contained the bread and cheese her mother had left for her. Benjamin looked in the direction she had pointed.

"Pick it up and get out of here, NOW!"

She grabbed it quickly and left with one scared backward glance at her brother. Although her brother was only four years older than she was, she was now terrified of him.

10

Night of nights

The next day was Thursday and she and Martha had planned to meet on the beach at eight o'clock to watch the men catch turtles. Martha had apologized for not turning up to the picnic saying that her father would not allow her to leave the stall. She was trying to make up for not meeting with her for the picnic as they had planned.

She could hear her mother in the kitchen singing whilst she prepared food for her lunch. She knew that Benjamin had already left for work, because she could see his cot leaning against the wall next to the bed. Thursday was the best day, because her mother left early in the morning and didn't return until night, so she would have all day and most of the night to do whatever she wished. Benjamin was supposed to keep an eye on her, but he usually went off with his friends, after taking her to their Aunt's house. He would watch her walk up the track to the house but he never waited to make sure that she actually went through the door. However, tonight was going to be different.

Sandra could now hear her mother moving about in the sitting room. Another voice had joined her mother's and this voice was angry. They were both shouting. Her mother's voice was the louder of the two. She was shouting and using profanity as she usually did. Sandra covered her ears with her hands. She only heard what her father refer to as 'rude words' when she was visiting her mother. All these relatives, including her brother, used them regularly; bad language was part of their regular vocabulary. Even her cousins Annie and Mildred used foul language and they were only twelve and fifteen. They would laugh at her when she told them they should stop using 'rude words'.

Sandra heard the front door slam shut, followed by her mother muttering. She heard her mother say, ",...and tell her to stay away from my fucking house."

"I don't know why he's so eager to be a pussy man, and why her?" She stupsed. She peeped her head into the bedroom and announced.

"Sandra, Sandra. I'm leaving now. You take care today. I will be home by half past ten. Keep away from the water and those boys who hang around down there. Don't do them any favours, you're not ready yet...besides, I don't want to have to explain anything to your Father." She warned.

"O.K. Ma," she replied. After she heard the front door close, she sighed.

Now, she thought *I can continue to read my book*. Minutes later, there was a knock at the door and almost simultaneously, it opened. She knew the voices immediately. They belonged to her two cousins, Annie and Mildred. They rushed into the bedroom, shouting her name. Annie immediately jumped on the bed and began jumping up and down, as if she was on a trampoline.

"Stop! Stop!' Mildred screeched. "Get off the fucking bed, you."

She gripped Annie by one arm and pulled her off the bed. She fell in a heap on the wooden floor with a loud thud. Annie began to cry loudly. She was holding her right arm.

"You hurt my arm. I'm going to tell," she said in between the sobs and she headed for the door.

"Come, Annie," Sandra said. "Come and lie next to me."

She patted the spot on the bed next to her. Annie turned and she lay down at the edge of the bed next to Sandra. Annie kissed her on the lips.

"That's what Mildred was doing last night with Mr Taylor." She said and laughed.

Mildred responded angrily.

"Shut up! Shut up! You talk too much."

She walked over to the bed and slapped Annie across the cheek. Annie didn't cry. She held onto her cheek.

"You did, you did. You did kiss him and you let him lie on top of you. I was watching."

Mildred moved towards her again, fury etched on her face. She walked closer to her sister, pulled her off the bed and began to shake her by the shoulders. Annie was screaming and was trying to pull herself away from her sister, but Mildred pushed her down onto the floor. She began to punch her in her stomach. Annie continued to scream at the top of her voice. The scene looked very similar to the fights that broke out quite frequently on the 'Strip' over men, women or fish.

Sandra looked at the two sisters as they fought. She was uncertain about what to do. She didn't want to pick a fight with Mildred. She knew if she took Annie's side that Mildred would attack her also: she had often seen her do that. She knew that if they got into a fight that she would lose. Mildred was much stronger that her and was accustomed to fighting. Sandra had never had a fight in her life. Nevertheless, she couldn't take Annie's weeping anymore and she sat up in the bed and shouted,

"Mildred, let her go. You're hurting her."

Mildred turned to face Sandra, while at the same time trying to keep her grip on Annie, but Annie was fighting to get away and with Sandra's intervention was able to wriggle free from her sister's grip and run out of the house. She left the door opened.

"Why don't you mind your own fucking business, Miss High and Mighty?" Mildred said sneeringly and ran out of the room after her sister.

Sandra heard a loud painful scream from outside. It was Annie voice. She jumped out of bed and rushed to the door. Annie was flat on her back on the ground. Mildred was stooping over her with one knee in her stomach. Mildred was slapping her continuously in the face. A few of the neighbourhood children were already gathered and were watching the two sisters. They were already drawing bets as to who was going to win the fight.

Suddenly, their mother, Susan, Sandra's Aunt appeared at her kitchen door with a bucket of water which she threw on both girls.

"Yu fight like fucking dogs, then yu get treated like them," she screamed.

"What the fuck!" Mildred exclaimed shocked. She immediately released Annie who had enough presence to punch her in the stomach. Both girls were now flat on their backs on the ground, wet shivering and breathing heavily.

Susan turned her attention to the crowd.

"Get yu asses out of here. There's nothing more to watch," she shouted and took a step in their direction. The children began to back away immediately.

Both girls were now in a sitting position on the ground looking menacingly at each other. Mildred was pulling at her wet clothes.

Annie was sobbing and rubbing her stomach.

"Oh, my chest hurt," she cried looking at her mother.

"Pick up the fucking bucket and bring me some water in the kitchen," Susan said pointing at Annie

Susan walked back to the kitchen door and waited there. She was watching her two daughters suspiciously. Mildred was the first to get on her feet and wagged a finger at Annie direction. She headed towards the kitchen where her mother was waiting. As Mildred walked passed her mother she thumped her at the back of her head with a fisted hand, saying angrily,

"I told yu, not to fight with yu sister."

Ow," Mildred howled as she stumbled into the kitchen.

Annie got up much more slowly, picked up the bucket and walking towards the pipe to catch the water.

Sandra watched watch the scene with her cousins knowing that the fight had not ended. She knew that Mildred would be plotting her next move to beat up Annie.

Sandra and Martha settled themselves behind a hedge of young sea grape trees. Thomas had promised to join them but he had had to go out with his father to visit a sick relative. Martha had brought a torch. However, they didn't need it because the moonlight was brilliant that night.

They had arrived early enough to see the first turtles emerge from the sea and slowly make their way up the beach in search of somewhere dark and quiet to lay their eggs. Sandra's heart was beating very hard. She had never seen a live turtle this close and she had to touch her chest in an attempt to calm herself.

They were huddled very close, and she could feel Martha's breath on her ear. It was impossible to see the turtles once they found the place chosen to lay their eggs, but they continued to watch as more and more of them ascended onto the beach. Martha had told her that they might have to wait for at least an hour for the men to arrive, so they stayed huddled together behind the hedge. Martha said that the men would wait until the turtles had laid their eggs and were returning to the water before they attempted to catch them. As they watched beach, they could see some of the turtles, start heading back to the water.

Then they heard the men's voices approaching from the opposite side of the beach. They carried torches, which they shone where the turtles were. The men all held large planks; one raised his and used it to hit the turtle that was closest to the water. The other men then joined in. They began to beat all the turtles as they made their slow trek towards the water.

Sandra cringed with each blow. She felt sorry for the animals because the logs were so huge. She ran from their hiding place, screaming at the top of her voice.

"Stop it! Stop it!"

She ran between the men and the turtles. One of the men shone a torch in her face so she covered her eyes from the glare.

"Move, you idiot," shouted another man with his log raised. "If you don't, I'll make sure you get this."

He pushed the log menacingly in Sandra's face.

"No Pa! No!" screamed Martha.

She ran toward Sandra and stood in front of her, facing her Father, Fred Clarke.

"Jesus Christ! What you doing here, girl?" he asked angrily.

He was looking at both the girls. He dropped his log to his side and looked around at the other men. No one said anything.

"It's...it's not her fault. I...I brought her here." Martha replied, stuttering.

Her hands were held up in front of her face as if in prayer. She intertwined her fingers nervously. She could see that her father was livid, and she knew what that meant. He might choose to beat her here, or he might wait until they got home, but no matter when it happened she knew that it was going to be brutal. The last time he had beaten her she could not go to school for a week. The other men remained quiet. They too were waiting to see what Fred Clarke would do. He was their leader and whatever he decided, they would do, acting in total agreement. They too, knew his temper and none of them wanted to confront him. They had seen too many men suffer because they had crossed Fred 'Iron' Clarke. They therefore waited patiently, but apprehensively, for his next instruction. He looked around at them again.

Frigging surfs, he thought. *Why I am surrounded by fucking fools?*

He looked towards the sea and noticed that the last remaining live turtles had escaped whilst they had been preoccupied with the girls. The turtles were now disappearing beneath the waves.

"Shit!" He exclaimed loudly. "Collect them," he ordered looking at the men and pointed to the three or four dead turtles.

"You cost me tonight, girl." Fred said pointing at Martha.

Neither Martha nor Sandra had moved. Sandra was wondering what was going to happen next. She had spotted how nervous Martha had become so had stepped back to stand by her rather than in front of her. She held her hands stretched out in front as if in prayer. Martha, however, remained completely still, her eyes darting from one man to another and then at Sandra, who had begun playing with her fingers nervously.

Fred Clarke was angry and Martha knew it. He took a step towards to girls and pointed at Sandra, his eyes glaring.

"You, get the hell out of here."

Sandra grabbed Martha hand.

"Not you." Fred said pointing at Martha.

He took a step closer to her and with his open palm slapped her on both sides of her face.

Sandra gasped in shock. He turned to her threateningly.

"Didn't you hear? Or do you want some?"

Spittle flew from his mouth; some was running down his chin. He wiped it with the back of his hand. He began to remove the belt from his waist.

"No, no Sir," she replied.

She looked at Martha. She already had both hands covering her face and was moaning quietly.

The belt came down between her shoulder blades twice and Martha began to scream. Sandra cringed. She was sure that after the second stroke, the belt had cut through Martha's thin dress. She could already see three or four shredded pieces hanging from what seemed to be a tear in the dress. Martha was crying loudly. At the same time, she was begging her father to stop, but he was not listening. The other men were laughing. Then Martha began to run and so did Sandra.

Sandra didn't stop running until she got into her mother's house. She pushed the door opened, panting very hard.

11

A new experience

"Where the fuck have you been?"

Her mother was looking at her, her eyes glaring and her mouth in its usual angry pout. Her mother was sitting at the dining table. She was not alone; there was an unknown man also sitting at the table on the opposite side of her.

He was red, tall and thin and had curly ginger hair. His arms and legs were extremely long; they were stretched out in front of him, blocking the doorway that led to the bedroom. He was looking at Sandra, rubbing his open palm across his chin and licking his lips.

"Leave the girl; can't you see she's frightened?" he demanded. He turned to give his full attention to Sandra. He was undressing her slowly.

“Come here, sweetheart,” he said slapping his huge palm on his lap. “Sit here and tell Uncle Taylor, where you’ve been.”

He stretched out both hands as if to embrace her. She stepped back, just out of reach. Sandra had never seen such large hands before. She looked at them nervously, not quite sure what to do. Her mother turned to him.

“You leave her alone. Isn’t Mildred enough for you?”

“OK! OK!” He replied waving his hands in the air.

Her mother was noticeably annoyed. She was still looking at Sandra, waiting for her answer, but Sandra didn’t know what to say.

“I asked you a fucking question, child. Where the hell were you?” She asked again.

This time more slowly and deliberately. Sandra was terrified. Her lips were trembling. She bit into the bottom one and tasted blood.

“You get into the bedroom. I’ll talk to you later.” Her mother said finally.

The next day, Friday, was the day her mother worked from home. Sandra was woken by her at about five-thirty. Her mother shook Sandra roughly.

“Get up and come and help me in the kitchen.”

They worked quietly. As they worked, her mother hummed to herself. She had assigned

Sandra to chop up onions. Within half an hour, Sandra's eyes were streaming and she had begun to sniffle. Her mother would look across from time-to-time. As yet, she had said nothing to Sandra regarding what had happened the previous night outing. Eventually, she asked calmly.

"And, where were you last night?"

"With, with, with Martha. Watching the men catch turtles." Sandra answered nervously, continuing to sniffer periodically.

"Her again! Listen you had better stay away from that young lady." She replied irritably, pointing the knife at Sandra.

"She spells trouble," she continued without any further explanation, but mumbled something that Sandra didn't hear.

"Hurry up with the onions. I need to get this done so that Susan can get it down to market..."

"Go and wake Mildred, I need her help to prepare the chicken."

Her mother and Aunt Susan had a food stall in the market at the weekends. Her mother prepared food for tourists, but mainly for the large influx of shoppers who frequented the market to do their weekly shop. Sandra and Mildred would usually help in the afternoons and early evening, taking orders, washing up dishes and clearing tables. Her mother had never asked her to help with the cooking before and Sandra began to wonder whether this was to be her punishment for staying out late the night before.

She arrived at her Aunt's house and shouted for Mildred and after hearing no response, entered the house. She knocked on the bedroom door that she knew Mildred shared with Annie and pushed it opened. Mildred was lying on the bed and there was a naked man next to her. They appeared to be fast asleep. Her legs were wrapped around the man, who was lying on his face, with his red buttocks exposed. The bodies looked odd together one dark and the other pale with legs so long that they were hanging off the end of the bed and one arm stretched the width of its heavy metal frame.

Sandra wondered what she would have to do wake up Mildred without having to go any closer to them. She turned her face back towards the door and shouted out her name. Both Mildred and the man stirred.

"Shit," Mildred said. She turned and stretched. The man yawned loudly. He too turned over on his back.

"Why is your face turned away, sweetheart?"

Sandra recognized the voice. It was the same man who had been at her mother's house the previous night.

"Why don't you come over here and the three of us can have some fun?"

"You leave her alone, Reds," Mildred replied, and nudged him in his ribs. "She's 'Miss Prim and Proper.'"

Sandra ignored both of them and delivered the message from her mother but kept her face facing the door. She left the room and closed the door behind her quietly.

Mildred watched Sandra's back as she spoke but said nothing. She got up off the bed, but Reds held her arm and pulled her back down.

"No Reds," Mildred said pulling away.

She slipped away from him and got up. This time he didn't try to pull her back. He yawned loudly again and she walked over to where her clothes were in a heap and began searching through them.

12

Returning to live in Coveville

The next year, at age thirteen, Sandra returned to her mother to live. Her grandmother had died soon after she had returned to the farm and her grandfather had followed her four months later. Soon after her grandfather died, her father told her that she would have to return to her mother because he and his wife had sold the farm and were migrating to Canada where his wife had relatives. He assured her that after they settled he would send for her.

When her mother heard this she remarked, "If it depends on his wife, he wouldn't send for you. She hated the idea that he took you to live with them."

Whatever her mother felt about her stepmother, Sandra was very unhappy at the turn of events. She was undecided about where she wanted to live. The last summer she had been in Coveville, things had changed. She used to love spending time with her mother, brother and other relatives. However, her brother had changed and she didn't want to live with him anymore. Additionally, there was tension or people who were constantly quarrelling or fighting.

This disappointment reminded her that there were things that she loved about the farm

She had begun to reflect on these things after her last summer away. At the farm there was plenty of food; she had her own bedroom and didn't have to share with anyone. In Coveville, there were nights when her mother ordered her to sleep with her cousins, Annie and Mildred. She didn't like sleeping with them, because there was hardly any room in the tiny bed they shared. She would therefore normally elect to sleep on the floor on some sheets. Her cousins had also changed and she no longer liked the way that they behaved.

Luckily this last summer, she had not had to sleep either on the floor or at her cousins. Her mother, who now had a job as a housekeeper, worked all day and most evenings and didn't return home until the early hours of the mornings. Sandra had her mother's bed to herself. She was left in her brother's custody.

She loved it when this happened. Her brother had other interests so that as long as she was home by the time he said, he didn't bother about where she was or what she was doing. He would simply warn her not to come home until the time he specified with the warning that if she did he would beat her.

She therefore spent time with Thomas at the beach swimming or fishing off the pier. She'd asked Thomas to teach her to swim and he had obliged. Her swimming skills had improved drastically and she was now able to dive into the sea from the pier.

In spite of this change, she had been glad to return to the farm at the end of the summer.

Thinking it through, Sandra realized that she liked things exactly as they were, living with her father on the farm for most of the year and spending the summer with her mother in Coveville. She wished it would continue forever. Especially now that her mother had a job that allowed her to sleep at home and spend her days with Thomas roaming on the beach or with Martha.

However, this was not to be. She returned to live in Coveville at the end of the school term. Her stepmother had left three months earlier and her father was due to leave soon. She knew that she would miss him. She hoped that her mother was wrong and that he would send for her. She wished that she could leave with him, especially after her mother informed her that Martha no longer lived with her father. She now moved to stay with her grandmother in the city. In addition she also learned that Thomas had gone away with his family for part of the summer. When she asked her mother what had happened to Martha, she seemed very eager to explain why Martha no longer lived in the village

Her mother smiled ruefully and informed her that Martha was pregnant and that her father had beaten Martha so badly that she had lost the baby.

Her mother noticing the look of shock on Sandra her face added that it was Benjamin, her brother, who had got Martha pregnant. Someone had seen Martha going into the house with Benjamin when she was supposed to be working on her father's fish stall.

Janet explained that Fred had regularly asked her not to let Martha frequent her house and to stop Benjamin from seeing her. In turn, she told Fred that there was nothing she could do and that, as far as she was concerned, it was Martha who should stay away from her son. Martha was to be found working as a maid for the hospital in the city.

"Good riddance to her," she announced at the end of her explanation. "All this time I thought she was your friend; instead she was fucking around with Benjamin."

"We're well rid of her. Well rid of her." She repeated the statement and looked directly at Sandra to gauge her response. "All this time she was supposed to be your friend." She continued shaking her head at Sandra. "Well rid of her."

She walked away from Sandra and into the kitchen. She shouted from the kitchen. "Don't you ever mention her name around here again."

Sandra was numb. She didn't know how to reply to anything that her mother had just said. She also felt betrayed by Martha. Her mother was right, because all this time she had thought that they were best friends. She was not even aware that Martha had been her brother's girlfriend. She was upset with him because he had not said anything to her either.

I suppose he thought me a child, she thought.

She wondered if Martha had been in the house with her brother that day when she had returned for her lunch. She remembered that she was supposed to meet her on the beach for a picnic that day and that Martha had never turned up. She remembered her excuse as being that she was doing something for her father, but now her mother was saying that she had been in the house with Benjamin.

That summer was the loneliest that Sandra had ever spent in the village. She missed Martha, even though she wondered if they could ever retain their friendship. She also missed Thomas because together they used to have so fun. Now she had no one with whom to sneak out at night to watch the nightlife on the 'strip'.

Luckily, her mother kept her busy in preparation for the new school term. She was taken to the headmaster for an interview, to the seamstress to be measured and fitted for her new uniform, and to the store in the city for the shoes, books and other equipment she needed. Her mother complained bitterly that her father had not given her enough money and that Sandra might need to take a summer job if she was to get everything that she needed to start school. She told Sandra that she had already spoken to several shop owners and that they were willing to give her a trial. Sandra was unhappy at this development, but she knew that it was a waste of time to protest. She knew that from now on she would have to do whatever her mother wished until her father sent for her. He had warned her of this before he left. She didn't want to do anything to jeopardize her chances of living in America.

A new grocery and haberdashery store had just opened in the village, and her mother found Sandra work there. Sandra's job was to weigh and pack sugar, flour and rice into one pound, two pound and three pound bags, and pack them onto the shelves. The work was easy but boring. The store was always busy and Sandra shared the job with another girl, Irene. They would work alternate days, except on Sundays when the store remained closed.

The manager told Sandra, that the store was one of a number the owners were building in the villages. The main branch, in the city, had been established many years ago. However, Sandra hardly ever went into the city, so she therefore knew little about the store.

She turned up for work the third Monday and almost bumped into Thomas coming out of the manager's office.

"You," they both said in unison.

"Do you work here as well?" Sandra asked surprised by his sudden appearance.

"Well, yes. It's my father's store," he responded looking around the store.

"Oh!" She said surprised. "I didn't know."

A number of the other workers were staring at them curiously. He was embarrassed.

"Lets' talk later," he said hurriedly.

He walked passed her and out the door of the store, which swung shut behind him.

She was very glad to see Thomas, and from his reaction, it looked as if he too was glad to see her. Nonetheless, this unexpected meeting made her realize just how little they knew about each other. They never discussed themselves or what their families did.

They didn't see each other for the next few days, but on Friday, he handed her a note asking that they meet that evening outside Martha's father's stall.

They began walking towards the pier automatically. As usual, they sat on the edge of the pier and dangled their feet over the side. Sandra told him that she had moved back to the village permanently and this made him very happy. He grabbed her by the shoulders and hugged her tight.

"Do you think she'll ever come back?" Sandra asked him when he eventually released her.

'Who?" Thomas asked. She looked at Thomas puzzled.

"Martha, of course," she replied.

He shook his head. "I don't know. I hope so."

They began discussing Martha. They both missed her very much. Thomas said they were like 'the three musketeers', only now, one of them was missing. Thomas told her that Martha had almost died and had had to spend a month in hospital. Her father had beaten her to within an inch of her life and the police had arrested him. However, Martha refused to admit that it was him who had beaten her, so they had to release him.

Sandra began to feel bad about the things that she had said earlier about Martha. She considered contacting her even though her mother had expressly forbidden it. She knew that she could try to do to so secretly. She asked Thomas for his help but he declined as he didn't want to get her into trouble.

That night, Sandra found out that the store belonged to Thomas's father and uncle. They had inherited the business from their parents. This was their first venture outside the city, and later that year they were planning to open another branch elsewhere.

They arranged to meet the next day so that they could spend the morning catching up on news. They could no longer spend the day together, as in the afternoons, Thomas helped in the store.

Thomas was fifteen and this was his last year at a private school. He would be going off to college the following year to study management so that he could return to help manage the business. He explained to Sandra that he really wanted to study engineering, not business, but he had to do what his parents wanted.

He asked what she wanted to do when she left school. However, Sandra just looked at him and shrugged because this was something that she had never considered. She didn't know. In her family the topic was never discussed. She, therefore, could not answer.

The rest of the summer went quickly once Thomas arrived on the scene. Before she knew it, it was time for school to begin. Her new school was very different from the one in the country. There were many more students; in her class alone, there were thirty.

Sandra was walking home with Annie after school that first day, when she heard someone shout her name. The voice was unmistakable: it was Thomas. He had not yet returned to school and had left work to walk her home. He offered to carry her bag. Both girls laughed when made the request. Sandra felt embarrassed and refused. That was the only time she did refuse. After that, whenever he finished school early, or had a day off he would ride his bicycle up to her school to meet her. They became inseparable. He taught her to ride his bicycle and they would either ride together or she would ride and he would walk beside her.

Her mother soon heard about Thomas from Annie and Mildred. Sandra was sure that she would disapprove and that she would have to explain to her that they were just friends. Instead, however, her mother encouraged her. She told her 'not to hold back', 'give him whatever he wants', 'this relationship could secure your future and mine too'; because 'your father is not going to send for you'.

Sandra wondered what she meant by 'whatever he wants'. She was scared to ask her.

She knew for sure that Mildred would be able to explain what her mother meant. She wondered if she should ask her.

Mildred was in her class but had made no effort to be friendly to her at school. For the first few days when she had felt strange, as if everyone was looking at her, pointing and whispering, she thought of speaking to Mildred to tell her how intimidated she was by some of the other students and to seek her help. However she changed her mind after she found out that the ones who were giving her such a rough time were Mildred's friends. Sandra soon learnt that the other students were scared of them. They were bullies and would force students to give them money or lunch each day. They would disappear from the class from time to time throughout the day. The teacher never seemed too concerned about their disappearance and reappearance a few hours later. Invariably someone would complain about them and they would be sent to the head teacher.

Sandra wondered how she could ask Mildred without having to tell her why she wanted to know. In the end she got the answer without having to ask her directly. Mildred. Two days later, Mildred cornered her at school. She dragged her into the toilet, where her other friends were waiting.

"Hello, Miss High and Mighty," they all said in chorus. They watched as Mildred pushed her against the wall and asked,

"Are you doing it yet?"

Mildred came closer to laughed in her face. Sandra pushed her in the chest. However Mildred pressed her harder into the wooden structure of the toilet. Sandra could feel splinters sticking into her back.

"So! What's your answer, High and Mighty?" Mildred said in a sing song voice.

The other three girls surrounded her.

Sandra's heart was pounding hard against her breast. Mildred and her friends had a reputation for bringing girls into the toilet and beating them up. She knew that she could not fight and win them if they decided to do the same thing to her. One of the girls, Lydia pushed her hand into Sandra's bosom. She squeezed her nibble. Sandra flinched because it hurt.

"Well?" Lydia asked. Did he? Did he?"

"What?" Sandra replied nervously.

She looked from one girl to the next wondering what their next move would. Suddenly Mildred released her, laughed and said.

"You know," and rotated her hips against Sandra's, "like me and Reds." She kissed her hard on the lips. "Like this."

She stepped back and looked at Sandra in the face. She released her walked away from her and added, “Come girls, she’s not worth it.”

As she was about to go through the door she looked back at Sandra who was fixing her uniform and said,

“If you don’t, I certainly will. He would be much easier than Reds.”

Sandra could hear the giggling of the girls through the closed door. She knew that it was a waste of time to complain. Mildred would get her one way or the other. She would try to avoid her as much as she could in the future.

Mildred was not her only problem. In fact, she was the least of the problems she would have to endure. Thomas’s parents were unhappy when they heard about the friendship. The watched the budding relationship with trepidation. Whenever they challenged Thomas, he simply assured them that Sandra was his friend. Nevertheless, like everyone else who had lived in this part of the country for some time, his parents were aware of the Daley's reputation, and felt that they could not sanction even a ‘friendship only’ relationship. They warned Thomas about it but he just laughed whenever his parents reprimanded him.

His parents had planned for Thomas to attend college locally. They changed that and began to plan for him to study abroad like his older brother. They were not going to allow this ‘relationship’ to develop where it could become a problem for them or their son.

13

Maureen - The Baby

Sandra herself didn't understand how it happened. She and Thomas used to meet on Friday evenings after school and go for long walks. Sometimes they would go for a swim; however, one day Thomas suggested that they went swimming in one of the secluded coves. To get there, they had to climb over some rocks at the southern end of the semi-circle, which formed "Half Moon Bay."

It all began very innocently. As they swam, they would try to 'duck' each other. Thomas tried to 'duck' Sandra and she wrestled with him to try to slip away – he grabbed her swimsuit and as she wriggled, both straps slip off causing her breasts to become exposed.

She turned away from him and tried to cover herself.

"I'm so sorry, but they are huge, just like the ones in the magazine," Thomas said excitedly.

He held her around the shoulder and turned her around to face him. She had successfully covered her breasts; however, one of the straps had broken.

They were both shocked and embarrassed. Thomas was staring at the hand she now held protectively over the broken strap. He could feel a tingling in his groin. It was the same feeling he got when he looked at his Dad's magazines, or when he and Martha played their games. She had never wanted to go too far because of Benjamin and now she was no longer available and though her cousin Norma had allowed him to touch her, it was nothing like the feeling he now had for Sandra.

Thomas was now almost eighteen years old and all kinds of women were throwing themselves at him, especially because his family was perceived to be 'rich'. These women were prepared to do anything to satisfy his sexual needs. Even Mildred had trapped him in the office at the store one day and offered herself to him. However, he didn't want any of them. Sandra was the one he had grown to love and it was Sandra that he wanted. He knew that he would have a battle on his hands with his parents as they had previously warned him that she would be unsuitable as a wife. They were now making plans for him to leave the island to study because they didn't want the relationship between them to become serious.

"Those are the kind of girls you practise on," his father had said to him smiling and winking.

"It's not like that, Dad," Thomas had responded.

Nevertheless, it was like that, he now realized. He had been fooling himself all along. He could not take his eyes of Sandra's breasts. They were large like the ones in magazines but they were more beautiful. These breasts were special. The tingling continued in his trunks and he reached down to touch the front of his trousers. He wanted to touch himself and rub it in the way he did in the comfort of his bedroom, but he could not get the relief he wanted. He wanted to hold his penis and move his hand up and down the shaft, but could not do so in front of Sandra. His lips began to tremble.

"Why are you staring at me like that?" Sandra finally asked.

She touched him with her other arm. He didn't answer immediately, but looked around to see if anyone else had seen what had happened. There was another couple in the water but their backs were turned obviously involved in their own antics.

"Oh!" he gasped, "Your breasts, they're huge, just like the ones in the magazines. Can I touch them, please?" he pleaded and removed her hand from the strap.

The breast immediately fell out. He looked at her for a reply. None came and he proceeded to touch the nipple, before gradually beginning to squeeze it. An involuntary gasp escaped from Sandra's lips. Thomas looked at her. Her eyes were closed and her lips were squeezed tight. He continued to massage one breast and then the other.

"This feels so good."

He could feel his penis continue to stiffen. He took Sandra by the hand and led her out of the water.

Sandra was pregnant. Thomas's parents were horrified, especially after Thomas told them that he wanted to marry Sandra and was asking their permission to do so. They told him that marriage was out of the question. They reminded him of their plans for him to study overseas and asked if he were prepared to sacrifice all that for some 'slut'. Thomas didn't have an answer for his parents, because if he was honest, he had not really thought the whole thing through. However, he didn't want to admit that that afternoon in the water had been a colossal mistake. What had happened was entirely his fault. Now, he wanted to make things right for Sandra.

Additionally, Benjamin's threats were beginning to cause dismay among family members. When Benjamin found out that Sandra was pregnant, he went straight to the store to look for Thomas. He had made it impossible for Thomas to go to work and Thomas' parents had to report him to the police. The police had threatened Benjamin with imprisonment if he didn't stay away. However, everyone in the village knew that Benjamin didn't fear the police. Janet too knew her son. He would wait for the right time to attack Thomas.

Janet was not appalled at the turn of events, however. She immediately started to plan how to capitalise on the pregnancy. She visited Thomas' parents' home to find out what they intended to do about her daughter who was now pregnant. She was not interested in whether Thomas would marry Sandra; she hoped that they would agree to a monthly allowance for Sandra and the child after it was born. She knew that they would want to avoid any scandal associated with an illegitimate child. Janet was sure that she would get what she wanted, even if it was just to protect Thomas from Benjamin's wrath, because Benjamin had threatened to beat him 'within an inch' of his life.

The family took a restraining order out against Benjamin to stop him from harming their son. In spite of this, Thomas's father secretly met with Janet and explained that he was prepared to give her money to pay for Sandra to have an abortion and a bonus if she asked her Benjamin not to interfere with Thomas. These plans were to be kept a secret from both Thomas and his wife and they arranged for Janet to let everyone know that Sandra had a miscarriage.

This Janet agreed to do. However, the abortion never took place. When Thomas's father questioned her two months later, Janet explained that she would not allow Sandra to get rid of her grandchild. She informed him that he should be glad that his son was still alive with all his limbs intact.

Thomas' mother had been planning to migrate to England to join her parents and siblings for some years. She should have done so years ago but had married and stayed with her husband because of the business. Now she discussed the plans with Thomas's father. She believed that this was the only way to get Thomas away from Sandra and her family. The father agreed that they should leave. They would sell their part of the business to the brother and leave as soon as the legal aspects of handing over the business was finalised.

With the threat to Thomas's life his father brought their plans to migrate forward and seven months later, they left. His father was prepared to forego the business, which he signed over to his brother, rather than let his son marry one of the village whores' daughter. At least that was the story that came back to Sandra and her mother.

In spite of all this, Thomas and Sandra retained their friendship. However, Thomas left for England before the birth of his daughter Maureen. Before leaving, he promised Sandra that he would send for her and the baby as soon as he earned enough money to do so.

14

Waiting in Vain

Many months passed before Sandra received the first correspondence from Thomas. Maureen was now nine months old. He said that England was different from what he had expected. He had wanted to go to work immediately to help her and the baby but his parents, he said, had refused to let him. Instead, he was studying to be a car mechanic, which meant that he would not be able to work for another year.

Additionally, his parents had forbidden him from ever writing to her. He could no longer ask them for money; his father said that they were not obliged to do anything more for her. This was because Janet had visited them asking for money which they gave expecting Sandra to have an abortion. They were therefore not prepared to help because there should never have been a child. He had to ask whether she knew about this, but he apologized and again promised that as soon as he began to work, he would save up and send for both her and the baby.

Sandra cried when she received this letter. She showed it to her mother, but Janet refused to confirm whether she had received any money from Thomas's father. Instead she turned on Sandra angrily. She told her that what she did was no one's business.

"And you don't fucking question me, because they've deserted you, not me!"

Her mother was right once again. First her father and now Thomas had deserted and disappointed her. She had given up on her father, but she remained hopeful that Thomas would still keep his promise.

A year after her father left, he had written to say that he could no longer send for her. His explanation was that he and his wife were going through difficult times and that she had left him. He had promised that he would support her as much as he could. At least he did until he found out that she was pregnant.

When he heard that news, he wrote a very harsh letter to her mother. He also wrote to Sandra saying that he wanted nothing more to do with her. Since then he had not contacted her. She had written to her father to beg his forgiveness – she explained that it had been terrible mistake and now needed help. Months later, she was still waiting for a reply. Sandra now believed that she would never hear from her father again, but she was determined to wait for Thomas, no matter how long it took.

Two weeks later another letter came from England. This time from Thomas's father, in it he enclosed a postal order for £2 'for the child'. He begged Sandra to forget his son. He said that Thomas now had an opportunity to make a good life for himself. He suggested that there would be 'many men who would desire your kind of talent'. He promised that if she didn't contact Thomas again he would send her money every month for the child. He said that he could also make arrangements for his brother to provide the child with a monthly allowance of food. However, he insisted that was not to contact Thomas again.

How dare he? She thought. *We love each other*. Sandra cried herself to sleep that night cradling the baby in her arms. Sandra threw the letter aside after reading it, and began to cry. Her mother came into the bedroom when she heard her crying and picked up the letter.

"Bastard," she exclaimed sharply, I'll deal with this shit."

She walked out of the room with the letter in hand. Sandra didn't care, or wanted to know what her mother did. Months passed and she still heard nothing from Thomas. Sandra didn't know what to do. She wasn't really trained to do anything. In fact, she was turned away from school after having her baby. When the Principal discovered that, she was pregnant; her mother was asked to keep her at home, "because she was a bad influence on the other students". He added that she was not to return "afterwards either".

She was so confused, and wondered if she was wasting her time waiting for Thomas, whom she had not heard from for over a year. Her only work experience had been working in the store on Saturdays but that stopped as soon as they found out her baby was Thomas's. She wished that she could return to school or attend college and learn a skill.

Annie was now doing dressmaking and culinary arts. At sixteen years old, her only opportunities were being a maid, a shop assistant or being a labourer on one of the local farms. Regardless, whether she went to train or got a job, she would have to find someone to take care of the baby. Should she do as her mother has suggested, and find a man who could support her and Maureen? What if she became pregnant and then heard from Thomas? She didn't know what to do or whom she could turn to.

After Thomas left, many men in the district approached her, like ants drawn to sugar. They promised her heaven, earth, and everything in between if she went out with them. Her mother also invited men to the house in the hope that she would be interested in them. Her mother was adding pressure by saying that she would soon need help with rent and food; the money she was earning could not support all three of them.

"Any of these men would help you pay the rent," her mother had insisted. "Besides I'm tired of having to share my bedroom. I want my privacy back."

Sandra fell into a state a depression. She lost her appetite; she was constantly tired and had difficulty sleeping. She didn't know whether help would come. However, help came. She was still in bed that afternoon when there was a knock on the door. It was Annie and as usual she didn't wait for her to answer but pushed the door open. She had seen a notice on a market stall offering a job.

"I'll stay with Maureen and you can go and find out about it." Annie told her.

Sandra arrived at the stall at the same time as another much older woman, who was also looking for a job. The owner looked at both of them for about five minutes and then chose her.

"Be here tomorrow at 10 o'clock sharp." She said.

Sandra rushed back to the house to thank Annie. She then remembered Maureen. However, Annie had anticipated her thoughts.

"Mildred can keep her until I get home from school or Aunt Sandra gets home."

Sandra began work the next day. She worked from ten o'clock to five o'clock each day except Wednesdays when she worked half a day. The money was not much. She was glad that Mildred could take care of Maureen, because she certainly could not afford to pay someone to do so.

Unfortunately, one evening she came home earlier than usual and found Maureen playing outside in the dirt. She couldn't see Mildred anywhere so she walked into the house and heard groaning and grunting coming from her Aunt's bedroom. She didn't knock but tried the door. It was locked. The grunting and groaning was so loud that she was sure no one in the room would have heard the door.

She walked back to her mother's house with Maureen. She was angry, but she would deal with Mildred later. She wished she could make a break from her family. She didn't want her daughter growing up in that type of environment. She was tired of being accosted by the many men who visited the four tiny houses where the Daley's lived. She would love to leave her mother's house and the cramped conditions that they lived in. Her mother was right. There was no privacy for either of them. She wondered if she could ever get away. She prayed day and night to find a job that would help her to get away.

However, with little money and a job that paid very little, she had no choice, but to leave Maureen with Mildred, but she really needed Mildred to do a better job of taking care of her daughter.

15

Brother betrayal

A letter came from Thomas six months after the first. Sandra was surprised that he had written after his father's letter. He wrote that he had been studying hard, and had taken a part time job and would therefore begin to send her money the following month. Sandra assumed that Thomas was unaware of his father's letter and proposal. She decided not to speak to him about it.

His letters continued as did his money. It was not as much as she had hoped, but at least he was in touch, and with her job she was managing to make ends meet. Correspondence continued for eighteen months, by which time he had finished his course and had begun to work full-time.

Sandra felt it was time to ask how his plans were coming along for them joining him in

England. He said that he was saving and that he would need to find a suitable place for them to live. He suggested that she should come first and that Maureen, who was now three years old, would join them a few months later.

Another year passed, and though his letters still arrived, they were becoming less frequent, and more brief. He no longer shared his life with her.

Since this whole sorry situation had taken hold, Benjamin, her brother had derided her at every opportunity. He had changed into a monster and would find every opportunity to taunt her. He told her that she was not special as both her father and Thomas had dumped her. He told her that Thomas only wanted her for sex and that his family would never let them marry. He asked why she didn't find herself a regular man like Mildred or Annie, both of whom were being supported by well-to-do-men. Mildred had three children and had moved into a place of her own paid for by the father of her last child. Annie still lived with her mother but was pregnant with her second child.

After not hearing from Thomas for some time, Sandra was beginning to convince herself that Benjamin must be right. Perhaps her family background was preventing her from becoming the type of person she had planned for herself. Two weeks after his latest outburst, Benjamin came home drunk and stumbled into the bedroom that she shared with her mother and Maureen. Her mother was working nights so only Sandra and Maureen were home. He called her name, and she didn't answer. She didn't want another quarrel.

He got into bed with them and began to fondle Sandra. She tried to stop him but he continued unabated.

"I watch you walking around this house, as if you're some princess," he retorted angrily. "I'll show you tonight. You saving yu'self for Thomas", he mimicked continuing to pull at her nightgown.

"Please, you'll wake Maureen," she pleaded. "Come onto the floor then," he retorted.

He grabbed both of her hands in his one hand.

"No! No! Please leave me alone," she continued to beg.

She tried to pull her hands away from his vice-like grip. It was no use. Benjamin was big and strong. He dragged her off the bed and she fell on her back on the floor. He straddled her, and put one hand over her mouth.

"If you make a sound, I'll do Maureen as well."

He removed the hand and raised her nightgown. She never slept in panties, so it was easy. She squeezed her legs together, and he tried to prise her them apart.

"Open your legs," he ordered, and after a fight she obeyed. However, she continued to plead with him, but he had stopped listening.

He must have been planning this for some time, she thought.

"I'll hurt you and then make sure Thomas knows that you are a whore."

She was sobbing quietly. She didn't want to wake Maureen. She didn't want her to get hurt. Before she knew what was happening he was inside her.

"Move with me baby, move with me baby," he repeated as he moved up and down on top of her. She stayed underneath stubbornly refusing to move. He raised his hand, as if to slap her.

"Move I say, move. Let's both enjoy it." He continued to taunt her. "Do it for me or I'll do it to your daughter."

He raised his hand again and this time did slap her. She began to move. He continued to slap her and with each slap, her movements became more rapid, until he reached a crescendo and collapsed on top of her. She slid from underneath him. He was breathing hard. She wanted to leave the room to wash his smell off her, but she didn't want to leave Maureen in the room with him. She grabbed her up and rushed out. Maureen was moaning. As she left, Sandra locked the bedroom door, to make sure that even if Benjamin woke up he could not follow them.

"Sssssshhh."

She tried to settle Maureen as she rushed outside. She placed her down on the dirt floor. Maureen struggled and rubbed her eyes. Sandra washed herself off under the tap. Her face was burning from the slapping, but she would have to wait until the morning to see what it looked like.

She had also dragged the sheets off the bed when she left the room and she now used these to wrap herself and her daughter. They spent the rest of the night in her mother's kitchen.

Sandra was woken by someone shaking her shoulders. She looked up and saw her brother standing over her. He was already dressed for work. She looked around hurriedly for Maureen but she was still fast asleep next to her.

"It's alright," he began apologetically. "I'm not going to hurt her. I'm very sorry about last night. I didn't mean to harm you or Maureen and I'll never touch you in that way again."

He stretched out his hands towards her and she shrank away. She started to shake. He had hurt her last night, and now he was saying he was sorry. He walked away from her to the other side of the kitchen.

"You can't tell Mam about what happened."

It sounded like a threat. Sandra didn't reply. Her cheeks were aching so she reached up and touched the right one and then the left. She tried to open her mouth, but it hurt.

He turned sharply to glare at her.

"If you do it will be all round the town in no time, and sooner or later your fiancée will hear about it."

He stared at Sandra, who was cowering in the corner. From time to time, she would massage a cheek with her hands. She seemed to be in a world of her own, so he continued to speak.

"You can go back to the bedroom."

He headed towards the kitchen door. As he reached the door, he turned.

"By the way, you forgot that there was a spare key in the bedroom."

He was gone.

He didn't have to tell her not to tell her mother; Sandra knew that she could not tell anyone, least of all her. Janet would deal with Benjamin very harshly and then it would get out and someone would tell Thomas.

She had to find an excuse for her swollen face, however. She told everyone, including Mrs Evelyn, the owner of the stall, that she had a bad tooth and had to visit the dentist to have it extracted. She was absent from work for two days.

Unsurprisingly, Benjamin didn't keep his promise to stop. He knew when their mother worked nights. On those nights, he would leave his cot in the living room and come into the bedroom. So far it had happened six times and she knew it would continue unless she did something about it.

Sandra's biggest fear was Benjamin's threat that he would do 'it' to Maureen, if she didn't let him have her. Sandra knew that she would do anything to protect her daughter. She also realized for the first time that perhaps her family was right when they said that Thomas would never send for her.

"Hello, Sandra."

Sandra recognized the voice straight away. It was two days after her most recent encounter with Benjamin. It was Martha and she was standing in front of the stall smiling at her. Sandra stared at her not knowing what to say.

"Well." Martha said and stretched her hands "Aren't you glad to see me?"

So many emotions welled up inside Sandra and tears began to flow. Martha came around the counter and hugged her. She too began to cry.

"What's with this reunion?"

They turned to see Fred Clarke standing looking at them. He gave Sandra a look of contempt.

"I thought you were going to buy bread."

"I am. I did," Martha replied.

She looked nervous. It was the same look as the night that they disturbed the men catching turtles. Fred had a note in his hand and handed it to Martha.

"I chased after you to give you this,' he said, "I thought it might be important."

Martha took the letter from him and looked at the address. Suddenly her countenance changed.

"Yes, it is. Thanks."

He continued to stare at her.

"Well?"

"Dad, I will speak to Sandra if I like. You can't stop me anymore," she replied defiantly.

She looked at Sandra.

"Sandra, I'll talk to you later."

Martha walked up the strip in the direction of the bread shop, with her father walking slowly behind her like her security guard.

16

No hiding place

Sandra and Martha met later that evening outside her father's stall. He looked over at them from time to time, but didn't disturb them. Sandra wondered what had changed in Martha and her father's relationship. Martha was fussing over Maureen whom she was seeing for the first time, while Sandra explained what had happened to her since she went away.

"She looks like Thomas," she was saying.

She looked at Sandra and asked. "How are things between you two?"

Sandra explained. Martha was disappointed in Thomas, but didn't believe he would leave her stranded. After all, he told her about Maureen, as she and Thomas had kept in contact, but she had not heard from him for about two years.

She apologized to Sandra for not keeping in touch. However, she had almost died, because her father had beaten her so badly and things became difficult for her after she went to live with her grandmother. Her father had banned her from having anything to do with the Daley family, but refused to say why. She believed that her grandmother knew the reason, but she would not tell her either. She had taken her in on the one condition that she had no contact with the Daley's. Martha had to agree. However, Thomas kept her up-to-date with the village.

Martha also told Sandra what had happened between her and Benjamin. She said that they had been fooling about and yes, she had been at the house that day when Sandra had returned for lunch. She had wanted to tell Sandra, but Benjamin had threatened her with violence if she did. She was already scared of him by then.

Since she had returned to the village he had been regularly calling at the house. He would stand outside and shout her name, especially late in the evenings after his usual drinking binge. He said that he wanted her back: he wanted them to get married. Her father had called the police on many occasions and Martha looked at Sandra solemnly.

"But you know how it is with Benjamin. He doesn't fear the police. He just laughed at my father."

Benjamin had last been to her house two days ago. Eventually, she went out and told him that if he wished to see her he would have to stop drinking and come to see her when he was sober. He had left and she had not seen him since. She told Sandra that she cared for him but said that if they were to have a relationship it would have to be different from the one they had had before. She now had two children and didn't want to have a man like Benjamin around them.

"But the weekend is coming up, so we'll see."

They had been talking for three hours now. Maureen had slept and woken up and now was very restless. Darkness was beginning to settle in and around the Strip. The shopkeepers were beginning to light lanterns and electric lights. Sandra knew it was time for her to leave and Maureen was pulling at her hand impatiently.

However, she needed to discuss her situation with Martha. Martha didn't agree that she should do as her mother advised and find a man to take care of her and Maureen. She said that Sandra should continue to wait.

"Besides, you can now leave her with me," Martha announced excitedly.

"What do you mean?" Sandra asked.

Martha explained that the letter her father had given to earlier that morning was the qualification that she needed to begin her day care centre. She had done the course at the college in town and the letter was informing her that had been successful. She could now set up the nursery school as she had always dreamed at the back of her father's house, where the locals could leave their children, when they went to work. She had already spoken to Annie about helping her run the school and she had agreed. She suggested that Sandra should continue to work and wait until Thomas sent for them, because she would take care of Maureen.

Sandra was glad that Martha was back in her life, because she now had someone whom she could trust to take care of Maureen whilst she was at work and someone to offer her advice when she required it.

Once again, she wrote to Thomas to ask how soon they would be joining him. She needed to know how soon they could get out of Benjamin's way.

Further she wanted to prove both her mother and Benjamin wrong. Thomas loved her and was prepared to marry her, no matter what his parents wished.

The reply she received a month later was not what she had expected. The contents of the letter broke her heart. Thomas began by saying that he was getting married. He was sorry he had not told her that he had been seeing some else. His father had shown him her mother's letter stating that "Sandra wanted to move on and no longer wanted him in her life". He thanked her for her patience and promised that he would always love her and would continue to support Maureen.

She showed the letter to her mother. Janet didn't deny writing to Thomas's father. She laughed hollowly and explained that "those types never marry people like us. You're better off without him, mark my words".

Sandra knew that there was no point arguing with her mother, or in convincing Thomas, that her mother was wrong. Her mother, Benjamin, and Thomas's father had plotted against her and they had won. She would no longer build her hopes on anyone else's promise.

She recalled what Thomas's father had said the day that Thomas had introduced her to him. He had turned away and whispered under his breath.

"My God, have sex with her, but don't have to marry her. Those types you practise on."

She should have realized then that marriage was out of the question, in spite of all of Thomas' promises.

Now she also had to get away from Benjamin's vicious assaults. Moving to England had been her escape plan, but that was no longer an option. She had to take charge of her future and that of her daughter. She would do everything to make sure that no one else could harm them ever again. To do so she would need to make enough money so get her out of her current predicament.

She couldn't remember if Thomas had promised to support Maureen, but she no longer cared. She regretted waiting for Thomas, now that she had been betrayed. She reflected on the time she had wasted. She could have made enough money to buy timber to add a room to her mother's house by now, if she had followed her mother's plans.

Sandra stayed up that night working on her plan. She had to forget Thomas as he was no longer available. Maureen was now four years old and she had to do something that would secure their future. Her mother had spoken about a housekeeping job with 'Reds' Taylor the previous week. He had asked for her specifically. At the time, she had told her mother that she was not interested.

Now, however, she has changed her mind.

17

Gaining independence

Sandra had heard the rumours about 'Reds' Taylor being attacked and being seriously ill, but had been too caught up with her own problems to listen to the gossip. However, her mother filled her in after she had told her about the possibility of working for him.

Reds had met with a mysterious accident and both his legs had been broken. No one seemed to know exactly how it had happened. But, the rumours said that there had been a fight between him and his wife's brother, who was now in police custody charged with attempted murder. His wife had since left him. His regular housekeeper was planning to leave shortly to work for his wife and he needed someone to take over.

Sandra made up her mind. She wanted the job and the next morning she informed her mother. Janet had arranged with Taylor that initially they would share the position until Sandra could handle it by herself. He agreed. Taylor suggested that they should both come to the house on the first day they were to begin work and then decide between them who would stay the evening.

When they arrived at the farm, Joseph, the manager, met them at the gate. He was on his way into the city but said that Taylor wanted them to come to his room as soon as they arrived. He was waiting for them on the bedroom balcony. They could see Taylor..., at least his head. He was looking in their direction. He waved.

Joseph gave Janet a set of keys, which she used to open the front door and they headed straight up to the balcony. Her mother seemed familiar with the house. She reminded Sandra that she too had been there before, but Sandra didn't remember anything about it.

Taylor's eyes opened wide when she and her mother stepped onto his bedroom balcony. He was sitting on a wheeled chair and had some papers in his hand. He rested them on the table next to him and he pushed himself closer to Sandra and Janet with an outstretched hand. They all shook hands.

Anthony 'Reds' Taylor looked quite different from the man she remembered with her cousin, Mildred that early morning.

"Miss Prim and Proper. How are you?"

He didn't wait for her to reply.

"Your mother, I hope, explained what was required by both of you. I'm sure?' he continued looking directly at Sandra.

Sandra looked at him and nodded. She hated the name 'Miss Prim and Proper'. She had not heard it in many years, in fact not since Mildred moved away. She was the only person who still called her that, but nowadays it was said with disregard.

"Yes, but we haven't decided how we will work, yet." Her mother replied, stressing 'yet'.

He looked impatiently at his watch, turned to her mother and announced.

"Well, at least for today, from what Joseph has been telling me, Mrs Clarke has left the house in a mess. So, I would suggest that, both of you work today and maybe...maybe Sandrine, or is it Sandra...what is your name again, can stay the night?

"Sandra," Janet replied quickly. "But, but," Sandra began to protest. "What about Maureen?"

"Who the hell is Maureen?" he asked nonchalantly.

"Her daughter," Janet replied quickly.

"Well why not bring her?" He replied. "You'll have your own room, of course."

He looked at Janet.

"Did you tell her about the other arrangements, Jan?"

They both looked at Sandra and Janet replied nervously.

"No, but I'm sure she understands. Don't you Sandra?"

"And, my, she looks as succulent as ever. I must say she's filled out quite nicely. I'm sorry I wasn't the first one to taste that honey of yours, but there's still time for us. Don't you think?"

He looked at Sandra and smirked.

Sandra nodded and shifted from leg to leg as he spoke.

"Come ladies, sit down, and let's talk business."

Janet showed Sandra around the house. They were shocked at how filthy it was. It seemed that Mrs Clarke had been concentrating on taking care of Taylor and not with the upkeep of the house. They spent the next several hours cleaning the main areas which would be in use: the main living room, Taylor's bedroom, the kitchen and the bedroom that Sandra would be using. This was a small bedroom next to Taylor's.

Sandra was glad that Taylor had acceded to her plea that Maureen should be with her, whenever she had to spend the night as she was concerned about her welfare whilst she away from her. She promised that Maureen would not interfere with her work and that; in the meantime she would find someone whom she could trust to keep the child at nights. She would continue to leave her with Martha during the days, but she was not too sure if Martha would be to keep her at night.

The schedule for his care was organised between Janet and Reds. Janet would work in the day for the first few weeks, until Sandra learnt how to prepare lunch and dinner for Joseph and Taylor. Sandra would work nights. Joseph stayed at the house at night and would give whatever assistance required by Sandra.

Sandra left her mother cooking lunch and returned home to pack some clothes for herself and Maureen. At least, for a short time, she would be safe from the groping hands of her brother. She could spend all day with Maureen and at nights she too would be safe.

When Sandra returned with Maureen, Janet was on the balcony saying her goodbyes to Taylor. She had arranged to get a lift with a friend and had to be at the gate by 6 o'clock. She touched her granddaughter on the cheek, moved towards the balcony door, glanced back inside before closing it, and said,

"Goodnight, see you in the morning."

"Goodnight," Reds and Sandra said in unison. Maureen said nothing but continued to look at her grandmother until she had disappeared down the long corridor.

Taylor listened to the receding footsteps of Janet on the wooden floor, then turned and asked Sandra.

"What time does she go to bed?"

"Soon, Sir" she replied looking at him nervously.

"No Sir" was his response. "Call me, Reds or Taylor, but not Sir." Sandra nodded; she had never been in his presence on her own. She was not sure how to speak to him, or how to address him.

They continued to watch Janet walking down the long driveway to the main gate of the estate and onto the main road that would take her home. Joseph appeared at the gate as she was about to go through it – they spoke for a while and then he closed the gate behind her. Taylor sighed, turned to her and said:

"Well, make sure she remains in bed, because I don't want any disturbances during the night..., apart from your groans." He winked lasciviously.

It was about ten o'clock when Sandra, assisted by Joseph, had finished putting Taylor to bed. She walked to her bedroom. She was thankful that Maureen was still fast asleep. She had her bath and quietly crept into bed next to her daughter, who was snoring softly. She was tired but could not sleep, thinking of all that had happened in the past few days. She felt lucky that she had landed this job. She was happy that both were out of reach of her brother, at least for now.

Sandra was awakened the next morning by light streaming through the window. Maureen was also shaking her saying that someone was knocking at the door and calling her name. Sandra jumped up immediately. She looked around the room, trying to remember where she was.

"Holy shit; I forgot," she said and jumped out of the bed.

She rushed to the door and opened it. Joseph was standing there.

"It's 5.30, He's waiting for you."

"Ok, thanks," she replied and turned back to put on the dress she had dropped on the chair.

"Where're you going Mammy, can I come too?" Maureen asked.

"No, no, she said hurriedly. "Stay here."

"But, I'm hungry."

"Just wait," she now whispered and placed her finger on her lips. "Go and lie down, I'll be back soon."

Taylor was sitting up in bed grimacing in pain. He was trying to flex his legs.

"Fetch me the medicine over there on the table. I should have taken some last night. In future, please remind me. Understand?"

He looked at her with a warning look in his eyes.

"Yes,"

She began to pour the dark liquid into the spoon. It was a reprimand, and Sandra noted it.

"Give me two, of those. The doctor is coming in later this morning, so I want to be cleaned up and dressed before he arrives."

"Do you want to eat before or after your bath?"

"I'll just have a wipe down this morning. For now come and lay next to me. I want to rest my head between those breasts. Maybe that will help the pain to go away."

"And, Maureen?" she asked hesitantly, looking at him.

"What about her?" he asked, seemingly annoyed. "Does she have large breasts also?"

He patted the spot on the bed next to him.

"Come here!" He commanded.

Sandra looked at the bedroom door that remained opened.

"You don't have to close it. I can do what I like in my house."

She lay down next to him on the bed and he laid his head on her lap.

"That's better," he said and raised one hand to touch one breast and then the other. He let out a long tired breath.

"Sandra, Sandra!" Her mother was shaking her awake. She looked around the room. It took a moment but she soon remembered where she was.

"Where's...?" she began to ask, but her mother interrupted.

"He's on the balcony waiting for the doctor."

Maureen was standing next to her mother. She looked at her questioningly. Sandra was trying to find the right words to her explain to her daughter why she was in Taylor's bed.

"She'll be fine," Jan said, looking from daughter to granddaughter.

She knew what was going through Sandra's mind. She waved her hands about the room and continued:

"This is about surviving and her life will be better for it."

Sandra sighed. She hoped that she was doing the right thing. She had yet to tell her daughter that they were no longer going to England to join her father. She continued to look at her daughter, as her mother continued to admonish her about believing that anything good could have come from her relationship with Thomas.

Maureen was watching her grandmother and Sandra could see tears welling in her eyes. She was four years old and very knowledgeable. Sandra was sure that she understood everything that her grandmother was saying. She jumped out of the bed, took Maureen by the hand and walked into her bedroom. Sandra whispered to her mother as she walked passed,

"I've not told her yet."

Her mother responded dismissively,

"And why not? Y'll have to tell her sooner or later."

18

No, not again

Two weeks at the job and already things had fallen into a routine. Sandra would come home each morning and take Maureen to Martha for the day. She would go home and rest in preparation for the night's work. Today, however, she was extremely tired because Reds had kept her up most of the night. It had been Joseph's night off so she had to do everything herself.

She arrived at the house and went straight into the bedroom. She stripped and got into bed naked. She didn't realize how tired she was. She was awakened by a grunting sound and an immense pressure on her back pressing her deep into the mattress. It was Benjamin. He was lying on top of her. She could feel his penis between her legs. He slapped her on her buttocks.

"Open your legs," he commanded.

"No," she said and tried to turn over. He rested both hands on her shoulders and pressed her further into the mattress.

"Come on," he said and slapped her hard on her buttocks. This time it was much harder. It hurts. She shrieked.

"Shut up, shut up," he said angrily and pushed her head into the pillow to muffle the shrill, loud, piercing cry of pain. Her buttocks felt as if they would explode. Benjamin was strong and Sandra knew it was a losing battle, so she did what he asked. He pushed a finger inside her vagina and then his penis followed.

"Aaaaaaahhhhhh," he moaned.

He pushed deeper and deeper inside her. Sandra was lying very still moaning quietly.

"Move, move I tell you."

He hit her again, but this time it was with his belt.

"Ouch!" Sandra cried out.

He pushed her head deeper into the pillow to deaden her sounds. She was suffocating. She didn't want to die. Slowly, very slowly, she began to move, not to please him but because she was being deprived of air.

"Faster, faster," he was screaming at her.

He continued to hit her with his belt around her shoulders. She begged him to stop. "Then move," he shouted adamantly continuing to lash her about her shoulders and back. The pain was too much for Sandra and she had to give in.

"You're the best," he said breathlessly. "I missed you last night. I saw when you dropped off Maureen. Yes, yes, much better. AHHHHHHHHHHHHHHHHH," he bawled out and collapsed on her back.

"That was really good," he said breathlessly. He shifted his position and lay next to her.

She could feel his semen running down her legs. She jumped out of the bed and rushed out of the bedroom to get the basin so that she could wash herself off. She felt disgusted.

He walked out of the bedroom buckling his belt as she returned into the house. He walked up very close to her. He was about a head taller than her and very muscular. He grabbed her by one hand and with the other he raised her chin so that she was looking in his face. She tried to pull away but he brushed her cheek with a gentle slap.

"I really don't want to hurt you," he warned.

"Then leave me alone," she pleaded.

"But, I can't. You will have to fuck Taylor at night, and fuck me in the day," he said with a smirk.

After he left the house, Sandra went back into the bedroom, and this time she locked the door. Just when she thought she was safe from Benjamin. It appeared that the only way she could be secure from Benjamin was not to return to the house. Therefore, Sandra decided to leave Maureen with Martha for the next few nights. There would be no need for her to return home and she would stay out of Benjamin's way. She didn't know how long her employment with Taylor would be, but she planned to save as much money as possible so that she could find somewhere else to live, away from Benjamin.

From that first night, Taylor had indicated what he expected from her and she was prepared to let him have it. She reasoned that she might as well do what he wanted and be paid for it, rather than let her brother get it free and abuse her in the process. Therefore, with Maureen now out of the way, Sandra was ready to do whatever Taylor wanted.

The night before when she had shown reluctance to join him on the bed he had told her that she was not obliged to do what he wished because he could find someone else. Sandra had no doubt that he would.

"Of course, we'd have to negotiate payment for those services." He had added.

Her mother was about to leave when she arrived at six o'clock. Sandra told her about her plans. She said nothing. She nodded her head and smiled.

"Just make sure he feels good and you'll be alright."

Three hours later, Sandra walked to the kitchen with Joseph. Supper was over, the dishes were washed and everything had been put away in the cupboard. All that was left to be done before they retired for the night was for Taylor to have his bath. Joseph took a huge bath pan up to Taylor's bedroom. He asked Sandra to boil water in several pans. The whole process took about twenty minutes.

"Joseph leave us now, I'll send Sandra for you if I wish to get in, or when we need more water."

Once Joseph left Taylor said to Sandra,

"Come in front I want to look at those breasts of yours."

Sandra moved in front of him.

"Take off your blouse," he demanded. "Like I said, I can get someone else, but your mother begged me to give you the job because you needed the money, so you can please yourself."

He turned away temporarily until he heard Sandra take off her blouse. Taylor's eyes almost pop out their sockets. Sandra began to take off his shirt and as she leaned over to do so, he placed one hand on one of her breasts, and when there was no complaint from Sandra, he placed his other hand on the other. Sandra still didn't move so he dug his hands into her brassiere and took both breasts out; they hung out of the brassiere.

"Nice, nice."

He continued to feel them whilst Sandra used the wet flannel to wipe his upper body. This lasted about three minutes.

"Come closer, I want to feel, to suck them. OWWWWWWWWW," he said. "The Daley women have the greatest breasts in all the lands."

He was groaning. He kissed one nipple, looked up at her face, and then kissed the other. He snuggled his head between Sandra's breasts. He was breathing heavily. He began to rub his crotch and Sandra could see the beginning of an erection. She knelt down in front of him and pulled down his trousers. She could see that he was bulging before the trousers fell to his knees. She gasped because she was not prepared for the size of his erection.

"Yes," he said. "It's big."

She took the towel and very gently began to wipe the bottom part of his body. She paid extra attention to his private parts, and he seemed to enjoy it, every so often he let out a groan.

Suddenly he said, "Wrap the towel around me; put back on your blouse, and call Joseph."

When Joseph arrived, Taylor ordered him to help him into bed. He did so and then left the room. Taylor then ordered Sandra to take off her clothes and use the water in the tub to bathe, whilst he watched her. He watched her as she used the flannel to wipe herself.

"Take a shirt from that drawer and put it on, then come over here and snuggle yourself up next to me, like you did this morning."

He patted the mattress. "Let me put my head between your breasts. Let me touch you and then...then...

"But, but," she began to protest and pointed to the door.

"Yes, I can see it, too. I told you this is my house." Three nights later they had sex for the first time. It was different with Taylor; she willingly did whatever he asked of her. This was the first time Sandra had actually enjoyed sex.

'Reds' Taylor instructed her on exactly what he wanted her to do. For an 'old' man, he knew how to give a woman pleasure. His legs apparently didn't hinder what he wished her to do. After he had spent himself and was panting heavily next to her in the bed, she wanted to beg him for more. Her whole body was on fire. She had never felt like this with Thomas. They had been far too young and inexperienced to know how to get pleasure from each other. It had simply been a very clumsy exploration of each other's body, and then she fell pregnant. They had hardly known what to do to give each other pleasure.

Apart from Thomas, only had her brother had touched her, and that had only given her plenty of unwanted pain. She hoped that she had seen the last of her brother. As much as she loved her village, he had made it too painful for her to want to live there anymore.

After a month, Sandra took over the housekeeping responsibilities from her mother. She was now a permanent resident in the house. She found it hard to manage at first, but she learned quickly how to handle all the cooking and cleaning whilst providing Taylor with all his needs.

Sandra quickly realized that he didn't like children, so she kept Maureen out of his way as much as possible. With the help of her mother, Martha and Joseph she was able to keep her out of his way.

9

The untimely death

Sandra worked with 'Reds' Taylor for eight months; he was now in financial trouble and would have to sell off most of his properties. Joseph explained that the family lawyers had hired him five years earlier to manage the properties because Taylor had made many bad investments. The houses and land had been in the family for generations. The properties included the land and houses where the Daley's lived in Coveville.

The seriousness of the situation only became clear after Taylor's wife left because thereafter he no longer had access to her money. He had tried to persuade her to return but instead she sought a divorce. Taylor's wife had found out how her money was being spent, so she got her brother to talk to Taylor, but they ended up fighting, instead of talking. His wife then left and took what was left of her money with her.

Joseph provided Sandra with the full information about what properties were for sale and where they were located. When she discovered that one of the areas was Coveville, she informed her mother and other relatives immediately.

She recommended clubbing together to buy the houses they currently lived in. However, they didn't take her seriously. Instead her mother suggested that she should put her money, hers and Benjamin's, to buy their plot and then she could add a room for herself, just as Benjamin was in the process of doing.

Understandably Sandra refused. However much she loved Coveville she could no longer live under the same roof as her brother. Besides, she had her own plans. She asked Joseph to let her know about all the properties for sale. With the money she had saved, she paid a deposit on a piece of land three miles outside Coveville.

Her mother and relatives were annoyed that she had chosen not to help the family and that she had chosen to move so far away. Sandra and her mother were now estranged. Janet had called her selfish for not sticking with her family. Sandra wished that she could tell her relatives the real reason why she had elected to move away.

However, she knew that they would not believe her, particularly, not her mother.

Eight months later Sandra found herself preparing to move out of Taylor's house. For the past three weeks, she had lived there alone. She had not seen Maureen in all that time and missed her terribly. She was looking forward to seeing her later that evening. She was also looking forward to catching up on village gossip with Martha.

Taylor had fully recovered from his injuries and had left for his father's house in the country. Joseph was travelling around the country tying up loose ends. She was not sure if she would ever see Taylor again. He was now a humbled man. She had watched him change from the arrogant, self-assured man she had met that first time in her mother's house, into someone who had lost his confidence and self-assurance.

Sandra had also changed. The once shy, timid, insecure girl was now a woman filled with self-confidence. Joseph had helped her to secure another housekeeping job with a good family, mother, father and four children. She would have her own room and Maureen could now live with her. She had been concerned about leaving Maureen with Martha, as she and Benjamin had begun to speak again. She still feared Benjamin and worried about what he could do to Maureen. Sandra was thankful that Fred Clarke had not allowed him to visit his house during the time that Maureen was staying with Martha.

Sandra had only seen Benjamin in the distance these past months and she had avoided eye contact with him. She was determined to stay away from him at all costs. In the meantime, she had arranged for Maureen to stay with Mildred and her children, instead of Martha as she usually did. Sandra had never anticipated trusting Mildred with her daughter, but Mildred had morphed into someone who took her responsibilities as a mother very seriously.

Sandra was in her bedroom packing her things. She glanced at the clock, and began to hurry. Joseph was taking her into the village where she was to pick up Maureen. They were going to stay with Mildred for the weekend. There was a knock at her door.

"It's Joseph," came a voice that Sandra recognised straight away.

"You're early." She announced and rushed to the door. There was a look of consternation on Joseph's face.

"What's wrong?" she asked frightened.

Her heart began to beat faster. She placed her hand over her heart in an effort to calm herself.

"It's your brother," he replied concerned, "He's been murdered."

"What?" she replied. She was in shock. "My God, no, what do you mean, How did it happen?"

She stepped back into the room and dropped onto the bed. She thought that she should be glad, relieved because he could never hurt her or Maureen again. She didn't expect to feel this level of distress. She was experiencing a whole mixture of emotions from great sadness to immense elation.

Joseph didn't reply immediately but instead looked at her curiously. He stepped closer thinking that perhaps she would become hysterical. He had imagined her being distraught and had prepared himself to hold her close to him to comfort her. However, as she continued to stare at him for his response, he thought that he saw her facial expression change from grief to a smirk if only for a fleeting second.

"I, I, I don't know," he replied.

He rubbed his hands together nervously and continued. "I heard he had some argument with Fred Clarke and he was pushed off the jetty."

Sandra heard the full story from Martha days later after her brother's funeral. Martha and Benjamin had continued their on-off relationship, without anything becoming too serious. She consistently told him that before she would consider him as a boyfriend again that he had to change the way he was behaving. The change had started. Two weeks later, she acceded to his wish to meet him at his house so that they could talk. She had tried to tell her father that she really did like Benjamin, but every time he shut her down and became very angry, refusing to listen. Benjamin had called at their house twice to speak to him, but Fred had threatened him with his cutlass.

The evening before Benjamin died she had arranged to meet him at Janet's house. When she got there, she could hear groans coming from Benjamin's room. She tried the door, but it was locked. She then heard rustling noises. She knocked at the door and shouted for Benjamin. He didn't answer. She became suspicious and walked around the corner to a place that she could see anyone if the door opened, but from where they would not see her.

Minutes later it did open and her daughter, Lucy stepped out. Martha stepped out in front of her.

"What the hell were you doing in there?" She asked a bemused and shocked Lucy.

Benjamin came to the door with a glass of liquid in his hand. He was dressed in his underpants only. Martha could see milky stains on the front.

"Oh, that was you. We were just having some fun," he said in a slurred, smirking voice.

Martha looked at him. She knew exactly what had gone on. Anger boiled up inside her. She turned back to her daughter.

"What did he do to you?" she screamed.

Martha stepped towards her daughter, held her by the shoulders and shook her. Lucy began to cry.

"I, I suck him. He, he gave me some of his drink, and ... and ... then he told me to suck him and ... and ... gave me these," she stuttered whilst bawling.

She held out her open hand and it contained some coins. Martha took them from her and threw them at Benjamin, saying,

"Don't you ever come near me or my family again, Ever!"

Benjamin looked at the money, as it tumbled to the ground with a jingling sound.

"What? What did I do wrong? You used to have fun doing the same thing."

Martha didn't reply. Her face was flushed with anger. She was breathing heavily and her head was beginning to get dizzy. She grabbed Lucy's hand and pulled her down the hill to her Father's house.

Her father was waiting for her when she arrived home. He had a large piece of metal pipe in his hand. He watched Martha as she approached.

"What happened?" he asked furiously.

She didn't know at that time that one of her father's friends had seen Lucy enter Benjamin's room; he was therefore planning to go up to the house to find out what was going on. Martha had little choice but to tell him what had happened.

Two hours later, Martha heard their neighbour shouting that her father was in a fight with Benjamin and that Benjamin had fallen over the pier.

By the time Martha arrived, Benjamin's body had already been retrieved and her father was in police custody. He had walked to the station after the incident and had handed himself in.

"But," Sandra said after hearing the story.

"He was such a good swimmer, why did he die?"

"He was drunk and when he fell he hit his head on the side of one of the boats tied to the jetty."

Both women went quiet. They were sitting in their usual spot on the rock overlooking the strip. Today, though, they had no time to admire the activities going on around them.

"What he did with Lucy, is exactly what he did with me that first time at your mother's house. You remember that day that you came back for your lunch?"

Martha continued. "He had said that he wanted me to see some magazines and then he wanted us to do what the people in the magazines were doing."

Martha looked at Sandra. They were both crying and in floods of tears.

"He was my brother, but he was bad,"

Sandra continued shaking her head, solemnly. "I thought many times about killing him myself."

Martha looked around at her sharply. "Why?"

Sandra told Martha about what her brother had done.

"No, no, no!" Martha wailed when Sandra finished. "I can't believe that you went through all that!"

"My mother is still vexed with Fred, but she doesn't know the truth. She doesn't know about this either, but I think it's time she was told. I think it's time I told her about Benjamin."

Days later Sandra was still trying to figure out how to tell her mother about the things that Benjamin had done. She visited her on her day off explaining that she had not seen Maureen for some time and that Maureen had been asking about her. In fact, it was true that Maureen had been asking about her "Gran" and Sandra had been finding all kinds of excuse for not allowing Maureen to visit her in Coveville.

When she arrived at the house both Janet and Maureen hugged and kissed each other.

Sandra watched them and shook her head. She thought that their greeting would never end. Janet had prepared food for them.

After they had eaten Sandra told Maureen to go outside to play so that she could talk to her mother. She left reluctantly, squeezing her Gran's hand lovely on her way out of the room.

Sandra told her mother what Martha said Benjamin had done to Lucy; she looked at her in disbelief. It was as if she was about to have an apoplectic fit. She was breathing sharply and rocking from side to side on the chair. She banged her fist on the table.

"What!" she eventually said. The words were spat at Sandra.

"That does not sound like your brother," she said shaking her head.

"They're making it up to make your brother look bad. He was not like that."

She was distraught. She leaned forward on the chair and looked Sandra in the eyes.

"Why are you listening to these lies? Jesus Christ, he was your brother, and Fred Clarke should be hung, drawn and quartered. Did Martha put you up to this?"

She was frantic. She slammed the table once again. This time Sandra jumped.

"Say something, damn you. Do you believe your brother did that?"

Janet was searching her face for an answer. When one didn't come she slumped back into the chair.

"So, so you believe her," Janet said resigned.

Sandra was becoming irate.

"Whether or not I believe what she said does not matter."

She looked across at her mother who had now quietened down.

"But I know what happened to me. "Let's see if you believe this."

Sandra related her own experiences with Benjamin. Janet looked at her from time to time with a blank expression as she heard how Benjamin had abused her over the years, the threats he had made towards Maureen and the reasons why she could never live in a house with him again.

All this talking had dredged up many buried emotions for Sandra. Towards the end she began to cry quietly. Janet listened and didn't interrupt Sandra with any questions or clarification. She got up from her stool and walked over to where Sandra was sitting.

"You finished?" she asked calmly.

Her voice lacked compassion. Sandra shook her head and continued to sniffle.

"Because...," she began, but Janet interrupted.

"Because you're a fucking liar, just like the rest of them," she screamed at Sandra. "A fucking liar, I don't believe you."

"But..., but...," Sandra tried to interject, but Janet would not let her speak.

She covered her ears and continued to scream at the top of her voice.

"You did something to make him do that to you. I don't want to hear you. My son . . .," she paused briefly. "He was not like that. I refuse to believe he did that to you. Now, get out of my fucking house."

20

Reconnecting

Sandra walked away from her mother's house that day promising never to see her again. She had always thought that Benjamin had been her mother's favourite child, and this confirmed it. Janet didn't really care about Sandra. She had fought Fred to keep Benjamin, but she had sent her to live with her father.

Sandra didn't see her mother for six months. Her new housekeeping job kept her out of the village. She maintained the family home and dropped and collected the three youngest children to and from school. Luckily, she was able to move Maureen into the same school. This made things much easier for her as she no longer had to ask Mildred to keep Maureen after school until she finished work.

Joseph was now part of her life as his wife had died. He would take Sandra and Maureen for long drives in the countryside at weekends. Sandra loved this respite, because it brought back memories of when she lived on the farm with her father. She would reminisce about her father and the life that she could have had. She often imagined what her life would have been like, if she had gone to live with him and his wife in America, or if they had not emigrated.

She might not have seen her mother, but that didn't mean she didn't hear about what she was doing. She heard about her latest conquests and occasional fights with her rivals from Martha, Mildred, Annie, or one of her aunts. However, they met one Sunday afternoon. Joseph, Sandra and Maureen had been on their way back home, when Maureen asked for ice cream.

Joseph suggested that they drive to Coveville to Mel's Palace, on the pier. He remembered Sandra telling him that Melrose Browne, the owner, made the best ice cream. When they arrived at the parlour, two people were sitting at one of the tables with their heads close together.

Maureen was the first person to recognize her grandmother. Janet was sitting with a mature man. She had an ice cream in her hand and the two of them ate from the same cone.

"Granny, Granny!" Maureen shouted.

She released her hand from Joseph's and ran to Janet and into her arms. They were hugging and talking at the same time. It was obvious that they were happy to see each other.

"Mam, it's Granny!" Maureen said excitedly.

Both Joseph and Sandra were surprised by this show of affection.

"Yes, I know," Janet replied and took a step closer to her mother.

"Hello." Janet said. Sandra didn't reply.

She was shaking with rage. Maureen came over to Sandra, held her hand, and began to drag her mother towards Janet.

"How are you?" Janet asked.

She returned to her ice cream, ignoring the fact that Sandra had not responded to her previous greeting. She turned to her companion.

"Meet my daughter, Sandra," she said nonchalantly.

"A beauty like her mother. Hallo," he replied.

He looked her up and down.

"John."

He stretched out his hand and Sandra shook it. Joseph walked up to the ice cream counter, after nodding his greeting in Janet's direction.

"I'll be there in a second, let me just finish this." Janet announced in Joseph's direction.

"Finish this," she said to her companion, and handed him what was left of the ice cream. She got up and walked behind the counter.

"What ice cream do you want Maureen?" Joseph asked.

"Vanilla!" Maureen replied.

"You?" he asked pointing at Sandra.

"Soursop for me, please."

"Always was your favourite," Janet announced, looking at Sandra.

"Soursop for me too," said Joseph.

The atmosphere was tense. Janet continued to speak. She was asking many questions. She would look to Sandra for answers, but only Maureen would reply. Joseph paid for the ice cream and Sandra began to walk back to their truck. Janet stood at the window and watched her back. She turned and realized that Joseph and Maureen had not followed her, but instead were sitting at one of the tables eating their ice cream. Janet joined them.

She had abandoned her companion, who seemed preoccupied with some other men who had joined him at his table. Sandra waited in the truck until they joined her.

"You are hard," Joseph whispered when they got in.

"You don't understand. Maybe one of these days I'll tell you about it." Sandra replied.

Over the next few years, the hostility between Sandra and Janet eased. Eventually they would speak, but it never returned to what it was. Sandra remained cautious around her mother.

They never spoke about her brother again. It was as if they had made a pact not to mention his name in any of their conversations.

Three years after that meeting at Mel's Parlour, Janet died. She was fifty-six years old. She had been involved in a fight with another woman, who accused her of taking her husband. The woman had knocked on Janet's door and when she had opened it, the woman with a knife in her hand, stabbed at her mother. Her mother managed to overpower her attacker and trap her on the ground until the police arrived. Both women were arrested and were later released with a warning. That night her mother died in her sleep. The post-mortem concluded that she had had a massive heart attack.

Weeks passed before Sandra went back to the house in the Coveville to clear her mother's things. The new owner had threatened to burn them if they were not taken out of the house. Sandra and Maureen were about to leave the house, when Maureen ran to her with a large collection of letters and other papers. She had found them underneath some loose floorboards.

Later that evening in her room, as she lay on her bed Sandra began to inspect the papers. Six of the letters were from Thomas's father in England. She read each one. They were terse. He merely mentioned *'find enclosed the money as promised, and I hope that you would keep your end of the bargain'*.

Sandra no longer had to wonder what her mother's end of the bargain was. It was all clear now. Her mother and Thomas's father had planned the break-up of her relationship with Thomas all along.

Her life, and Maureen's, would have been so much different, if only they had left things to take their natural course. She would not have had to spend her young life fighting off her brother's sexual advances, nor those of all the other men her mother had brought to her. Her mother had always known that there was not going to be a marriage between her and Thomas.

Sandra sighed, threw all the papers to the floor, and began to cry. She was crying not only for herself but also for her daughter and for Thomas. All this time, she had hated and despised him for deserting her. She had named him a coward for not standing up to his parents and now she knew that this was not true. Both of them had been manipulated by their parents.

This stirred up mixed feelings. The woman she was now wasn't what had been planned for her. She hadn't planned it herself and neither did her father. She recalled her fathers' words, when she first went to live with him. "I'm doing this because I don't want you to be like your mother, and the rest of them."

It was too late for her but what about her daughter?

.

21

The truth

Sandra was tidying the letters and other papers which she had strewn around the room the next morning, checking each as she picked it up.

One of them, written on a page from an exercise book, caught her attention. It began '*My dearest lover*'. Some of the handwriting was undecipherable and she could barely make out the signature. On scrutiny, she made out 'Fred Clarke'. It was a love letter.

She was stunned by the contents. It clearly explained the reason for Fred Clarke's hostility towards Benjamin and her mother. She read it several times that morning to make sure that what she was seeing was true. She would not be able to see Martha for four days to show her the letter. She had already taken a day off from work to clear out her mother's effects and she doubted whether she would be able to take another. She would have to wait until the weekend but was anxious to share the contents with her.

That Friday evening she sat with Martha on a bench outside her house looking over the letter. Martha stared at it in disbelief.

"So, that's why he didn't want me to have anything to do with Benjamin."

She looked at Sandra; her mouth gaping open.

"I can't believe it. He was my brother!" Martha shook her head. "Your mother was hard, cruel and single minded."

Sandra nodded in agreement. She had spent time reflecting on the letters from England that she had also found.

Yes, she thought. *She was, even to her children*.

"Are you going to say anything to your father?"

"I, I don't know. He's really suffering. He would've preferred it if they'd hanged him rather than serve him with a life sentence."

She turned to look at Sandra.

"He'll not survive in there, you know."

She shook her head. "It's now been five years."

There were tears in her eyes and as they dropped down on her cheeks, she didn't wipe them away.

"He wasn't always the best father; never paternal, but he always made sure that me and mamma had what we needed. I don't understand why your mother rejected him."

"I do," Sandra replied.

She said nothing more, because she didn't think that it was the right time to tell Martha her true feelings about her mother, or about her family.

"She really hurt him," Martha continued, breaking into Sandra's thoughts.

Martha held up the note in front of Sandra.

"He was begging her here to let him have the chance to raise his son. No," Martha said adamantly, "I can't say anything to him. Besides he might have forgotten about these things by now."

Fred Clarke hadn't forgotten. He had been tormented by Janet most of his life. He had relived every second as vividly as if were yesterday after Martha's last visit to tell him that Jan had died.

He and Janet had been friends and drinking partners. They were inseparable growing up. She, therefore, never took him seriously, until that night when they got drunk and had sex in his parent's bedroom. Thereafter, they had sex regularly. It was during the height of passion, one night that he had professed his love for her. She laughed at him.

"You can't afford me," she had said.

She then mentioned the other men who could give her money and gifts that Fred could not. "You're too poor. Let's just have fun."

Nevertheless, six weeks later she told him that she was pregnant and believed that it was his. He offered to marry her straight away but she refused. Instead she cursed him and told him to stay away from her.

It was at this point that he wrote the letter begging her to let him be a part of the child's life, even if she didn't marry him. However, this changed their relationship and it became very hostile.

Over the years, he had watched from a distance as Benjamin grew into a selfish, arrogant, self-opinioned young man. Fred knew that he needed a strong man to rein him in early and that Janet was never able to do so.

Additionally, her other activities interfered with the raising of a child. He remembered his own childhood and knew that if old Black Skerritt had not taken pity on him that he too would have gone down the wrong road. He had his demons and could see the same characteristics in Benjamin. He had therefore begged Clarence Smith to employ Benjamin as an apprentice in his boatyard, because, by age twelve, he was already known for being rude and a bully.

Fred was still in love with Janet, even after her degrading rejection. He didn't care about her faults although it was difficult to live in the same village with her chasing other men whom she felt could offer her more. Benjamin was also a constant reminder of what could have been. It had been very difficult to watch him grow up without having any say about his lifestyle choices.

God knows he hadn't intended to kill Benjamin. They had been in a violent argument. Fred was livid, but mostly with himself, because he felt that he should have done more, in spite of what Jan said. In his rage, he blurted out to Benjamin that he was his father and scolded him for not showing him more respect. Benjamin had simply looked at him, laughed in his face and with a look of disdain, said,

"You! You! You! A drunken coward like you! My father? You could never be my fucking father."

Benjamin spat in his face. That was the final humiliation for Fred. He pushed Benjamin in the chest and Benjamin grabbed his hand and they began to struggle. No one was giving in to the other. Eventually Benjamin slipped and fell into the water.

Fred had known for years that he should tell Martha the truth about Benjamin. However, he never built up the courage to do so. He didn't want his daughter to see him as a coward he was. All his bluster was simply to hide his inadequacies.

He would not have been able to deal with her rejection. Now, worse than that thought is that she hated him.

He was a defeated man. He covered his face with his hands. Initially his cries were quiet and muffled, the cry of a man hiding his pain. He knew it was too late. His cries eventually changed to dry hacking sobs which became both ferocious and noisy. He did not sleep well that night.

The next morning he asked the guard for pen and paper. Later that day they found him in his cell hanging from the roof. On his bed was a letter addressed to his daughter, Martha.

22

Making a new start

After the death of Fred, Sandra was ready to explain to Martha her ambivalent feelings about her family and in particular her mother, Janet.

Janet, she felt was never satisfied with what she had. She jumped at every opportunity to fulfil the elusive dreams that were in her head. Sandra had inherited the determination to succeed from her mother. However, she didn't believe that a dream could only be satisfied by selling yourself to the highest bidder, or at least to several men with perceived wealth.

Janet also believed that any children conceived because of these relationships, could be keep, given away, or a visit Ma Bates who would do what is necessary to get rid of it. Therefore, it was easy for to Janet to send Sandra to live with her father and for Benjamin to run wild around the village tormenting everyone and creating enemies for the whole family. Sandra doubted whether any of her female relatives had actually experienced love, which was why Janet had thrown scorn over Sandra's love for Thomas.

After Thomas and his family refused to provide the money as she had hoped, Janet's plan was to break the couple up and to find her daughter someone who could support her and the child, but only in such a way that she too could benefit.

Sandra began to reflect about her own behaviour towards men. She realized that she had inherited many of these family traits.

What now? She asked herself. *Is it too late to change?* She knew that whatever she decided to do in the future would affect her Maureen, or any other children she might have.

Five years after the death of her mother, Sandra was finally able to build a two bedroom wooden house with an inside bathroom and shower. It had taken her longer than she had anticipated, and she had used every avenue at her disposal to have it done.

She had lost Joseph. He was getting married soon. He had frequently proposed and each time she refused. Eventually he found someone who would marry him. They promised to remain friends, but their relationship had changed forever.

Again Sandra was job hunting. The Greens no longer needed her because the children had grown up and gone away to college. She was sorry to leave, but she didn't have to wait too long to find her perfect job. She was lucky to secure the position as there was stiff competition from Harriet Clarke and Betty Evans.

The three of them had turned up for the interview. She was the last person interviewed by Mary Payne, the wife of the couple. She felt sure that Betty would get the job because wives tended to choose women that their husband would not be attracted to. Sandra had lost out like this before, because of the way she looked. She was curvaceous and well-endowed but there was nothing she could do about this particular family trait. She was very surprised, therefore, when Mary told her that she had the job.

Once she heard the news, Sandra told Mary Payne that she had fourteen-year-old daughter, and had asked if she could come to the house each day to meet her after school. She brought Maureen with her when she visited to receive news about the job and left her on the balcony while Mary showed Sandra around the house. When they returned to the balcony, Maureen and Brendon Payne, Mary's husband, were sitting heads down looking at an open exercise book on the table in front of them. They looked up when Mary and Sandra arrived.

"Brendon, I didn't hear you arrive," Mary announced walking up to them.

"You have already met Maureen. This is her mother, Sandra Daley, who will be working for us."

Brendon was already on his feet. Sandra stood next to Maureen and offered her hand.

"Nice to meet you, Sir."

She nudged Maureen, who now got up and stretched out her hand.

"Nice to meet you, again," she said and smiled widely at Brendon, allowing her hand to linger extra long in his.

Sandra noticed Brendon's face. He was very busy ogling them both, but mostly Maureen. Maureen had been turning heads for some time now. Unwittingly she had spun her spell around the boys at school and they would fight to sit next her. She had complained that the only male teacher at the school would ask her to go to the blackboard work out the maths problems. Sandra smiled to herself. She knew why he had asked her to go to the board. It used to happen to her also. It was time to instruct her about men. She had been putting it off. However, Sandra had noticed of late that her male friends had started accidentally dropping by when they knew Maureen was alone in the house. Three months previously, Jim had called at the house to fix the 'broken window' that he had been promising to do for ages. He knew it was the one day that Maureen would be in the house for a few hours by herself. A few weeks later, Sandra had come home from to find Sam, her latest boyfriend, sitting on Maureen's bed showing her how to complete her homework. She therefore recognized the look she saw on Brendon's face.

Yes, she thought. *It is time for the talk.*

Brendon glared at the mother and daughter standing in front of him. He repeated to himself the words of Napoleon.

A beautiful woman, pleases the eye, a good woman pleases the heart; one is a jewel, the other a treasure.

Maureen though only fourteen, was already six foot five. Like her mother, she stood tall and statuesque, she shared Sandra's outstanding feature, like all 'Daley women', huge breasts. Both men and women admired them: the women wanted them and the men wanted to be wrapped in them.

Brendon felt a sudden jab in his side. It was his wife. She was standing next to him and had asked him a question and was waiting for him to respond. He was so engrossed ogling Sandra and Maureen, while at the same time trying to remember the exact words of Napoleon that he had stopped listening to what was going on around him.

"Brendon!" Mary repeated more loudly, nudging him again with her elbow. "Ms Daley asked if her daughter can come here straight from school and wait for her each evening."

She didn't need to turn to look at him, because she knew exactly what he was doing. She had been married to him for long enough. She had no doubt that he was drooling over the two females. Therefore, she too, kept her eyes firmly fixed on them. He caught himself quickly.

"Yes, sure," he replied nervously.

Mary had her reasons for choosing Sandra as a housekeeper. She was just the woman she needed around the house to keep Brendon away from her.

Well, maybe either would allow him to leave me alone, she thought. *I'm tired of his constant prodding. God knows I can't keep up with his sexual appetite.*

Moreover, she could return to see her parents without worrying about how he would take care of himself. He certainly wouldn't be experience the lack of sexual satisfaction that had been a feature of his life over the past few months.

"Thank you, Sir, I promise that she's a good girl," Sandra replied, patting Maureen on the shoulder.

Sure and already a flirt, Brendon thought, as Maureen fluttered her eyes demurely at him.

The last thing he wanted was for his wife to notice that the two beautiful dark-skinned women standing in front of them distracted him. They looked like sisters, not mother and daughter and he surmised that Sandra must have had Maureen when she was very young.

There was something magnetic about Maureen. She might be young, but she had the full figured body of a woman. He believed it was a fruit ripe enough to be plucked. Two hours later Brendon was back in his study. He could not take his mind off the two females he had just met. It was two months since his wife had let him touch her so he excused himself after they left so that he could relieve the pressure on his loins in the privacy of his study.

What beauties, he thought. *How will I keep my hands off them? Already my body is warming to the touch of those dark fingers. Those beautiful full ripe lips on my neck.*

"Oh! Oh!" he moaned as he relieved the pressure, and the white semen squirted on the towel he placed between his legs. He could not get his mind off Sandra and Maureen. He had qualms about Maureen being so young. However, from what he had observed, the girls in the islands matured much younger than in England. He was particularly interested in the daughter, but the mother would be just as good.

Those lovely breasts. I would love to have them wrapped around my face and hide my face in them. These island girls have something about them that the English do not, he thought.

An encounter with Sandra in the kitchen two days later decided him. He was trying to point out something to her in the kitchen, when he turned around suddenly and accidentally touched her on her breast. He apologized, but instead of being offended, she looked up at him, smiled provocatively and said, “Don’t worry about that.” He felt encouraged.

Days later he was still agonizing about how he could broach his thoughts with Mary. They had only been on the island for two months, but already she wanted to return to England to see her parents. In the last communication they had received, her father, who had always been sickly, had taken a turn for the worse. She was only hanging on here because they had no one to take care of the house if she left, but now that they had employed Sandra, she was free to return to England to be with her mother and ailing father for a while. Mary was thinking the same thing, but she wanted to make sure that Sandra could do the job she had employed her to do. So far, she was doing an excellent job.

Both Sandra and her daughter seemed to fit into the arrangement well. The daughter would call at the house each day after school and she would have dinner with her mother in the kitchen. The house settled into a pattern, and she told her husband that she was ready to return to England. She was not sure how long she would stay and so booked an open ticket. From what she had heard from the doctor attending to her father, they expected him to live for six months.

23

When the cat's away

With Mary out of the picture, Brendon set his plan into motion. He said that he didn't like eating alone and invited Sandra and Maureen to eat with him each day, instead of at the kitchen table. He also began to help Maureen with her homework. Each day after they had eaten they would disappear into his study whilst Sandra did the washing up. They would work together for an hour, or until Sandra would knock on the door to announce that she was ready to leave.

One day, Brendon arrived home earlier than usual. He had not been feeling well. He could not find Sandra in the kitchen or sitting room but then he heard a snore coming from the guest bedroom, so he decided to explore.

What a sight for sore eyes, he said to himself.

Sandra was lying on her back, across the bed, fast asleep. She was only dressed in her brassiere and panties and the brassiere only covered two-thirds of her breasts. He didn't want to awaken her, but he wanted to touch her breasts.

He stood over her and as he watched her chest heave, something happened inside him. The feverishness he had felt before entering the bedroom simply disappeared. He could not control himself and knelt down next to the bed, and pushed his hand underneath one of the bra cups and began playing with Sandra's nipple. He leaned over, kissed it and then began sucking on it.

Sandra groaned, shifted her position and opened her eyes. Initially she looked scared, but when she saw it was him, she simply said, "Oh! I'm sorry."

She neither covered up nor moved his hand which was still on her breast.

"Don't be scared," he said. "I just want to touch them. Please," he pleaded, "Take off the brassiere."

Sandra looked into his eyes and saw a man who needed her. He was rubbing his crotch and making those hissing noises that she recognized only too well. She knew exactly what he needed. Sandra had noticed from the first time that they had met that he could not keep his eyes off her or Maureen. She knew also that if he didn't get it from her, that he might approach Maureen. She would not have that so she needed to take care of the white man.

Sandra turned her back to him.

“You unhook it.”

Brendon unhooked the brassiere and when Sandra turned back to him and was about to take the straps from her shoulder, he stopped her and said, “I’ll do that.”

He very gently removed the left strap and then the right and gradually removed the brassiere. It fell into Sandra’s lap and her breasts fell free on her chest.

“Lovely, lovely,” Brendon hissed.

He was breathing heavily. He first touched the nipple of the left breast, then the right. He then placed both hands on the two breasts and squeezed them together. He continued to make the hissing sounds whispering, “Lovely, Lovely.”

He was on his knees in front of her and he kissed one breast, while squeezing the other. He bit each one in turn. Sandra let out a sharp groan. He looked up at her face, concerned.

“Sorry. This is heaven and you are my angel.”

He began to suck hard on the left breast, harder and harder as if he wanted to swallow it. He went from one to the next, squeezing, sucking, licking, biting. Sandra’s groans were growing louder. Suddenly he stopped looked at her and kissed her on the lips. He stood up in front of her took her hands and placed them on his crotch. Sandra felt his hardness. She didn't need to be told what to do. She unbuckled his belt and pulled down his zipper. His trousers fell to the floor and he stepped out of them.

Sandra was shocked at the paleness of his legs. She pushed her hand inside the slit of his underpants and released his penis. That too was very pale but was stiff and hard. She touched it and he let out a grunt. She stood up in front of him and as she pressed the full length of her body against his, they both groaned louder. He pushed her roughly back onto the bed and began to remove her panties. Five minutes later, it was over, and he was lying spent on the bed with his head resting between her breasts. They were both fast asleep.

They had sex every day after that, sometimes in the master bedroom, the guest room or the kitchen. However, they always made sure to finish before Maureen arrived from school.

Sandra was pregnant. The last time she had felt this queasy was fifteen years ago when she was expecting Maureen. Additionally, she had not bled for the past two months. Mary had seen Sandra rush from the kitchen to the yard. She followed and watched as she regurgitated her lunch. Mary looked at her with a knitted brow.

"What's the matter?" she asked nonchalantly. "You haven't been looking yourself recently. Are you were pregnant?"

Janet turned to face her. She could not lie.

"Yes," she replied.

She turned again because she could feel her stomach rumbling.

"When you have finished, come inside. We must talk." Minutes later, they were in the kitchen sitting opposite each other at the table. Sandra was nervous; she didn't want to lose this job.

Mary spoke first.

"Well! Is there something you should be telling me?" Sandra looked down at her hands but didn't speak. "

Well? Is the child my husband's? I know you have been having sex with him." She continued.

"Yes, yes."

Sandra got down on her knees in front of Mary.

"Please, I'll stop, but I can't lose this job. It's the best job I've ever had."

She grabbed Mary's knees. Mary removed her hands.

"Please get up; I'm sure you didn't seduce him."

Mary got up abruptly and walked towards the door leading to her bedroom. She turned to look at Sandra.

"Let me think about this," she said and slammed the door behind her.

Mary knew that she needed to show a level of repulsion and annoyance at what had happened. However, she was glad. She had fulfilled her plans, and it was a much easier than she had imagined.

"Yes! Yes!" she exclaimed excitedly, as she sat on the bed. She went into her drawer and took out some papers. She must begin to make the plans. She had both Brendon and Sandra exactly where she wanted them. Neither of them could disagree to the plans she had in mind.

When she had returned from England two months ago, she noticed straight away Brendon's relaxed state. He had not rushed her into the bedroom, stripped her naked and had sex with her as he usually did. He looked happy and was constantly humming. They had wanted a child and no matter how hard they had tried, it had proved impossible. They had applied to adopt, but had not been successful.

She therefore told Brendon what she had found out and the plans she wished to put in place to for them to adopt the child.

"At least it would have your blood," she said. "Well?"

Brendon had listened whilst she spoke. Initially he was shocked. He wished that he could deny what his wife allegations and suggestions, but he knew her. She always made sure of her facts before she planned. She had everything written out, including penalties, if the child turned out not to be his. He shrugged his shoulders.

"You can't fool me, Brendon Payne," she said and smiled at her husband. "I saw how you looked at them the first night you met them."

"And, you're not vexed?" He replied concerned.

"Not, if it meant leaving me alone." She replied, "It has worked out fine."

"But...," she paused. "I have to get something out of it," she continued smiling at her husband.

"So, who will speak to her?" he queried.

Sandra had been trying extra careful to make sure that she left no evidence when she and Brendon had sex. She had forgotten, however, that she should be taking care not to get pregnant. She could go to Ma Bates in the village and have it aborted, but that was not something her conscience would let her do. She could not bring herself to kill the child that was growing inside her. Mary had asked to speak to her as soon as she arrived at work the next morning. This made her nervous. She hoped that she wasn't going to lose the job. She had made a terrible mistake becoming pregnant.

Things have been going so well for both her and Maureen. Her work at school had improved tremendously since Brendon had begun to help her. Sandra had been able to save more money than she ever thought possible. She had actually begun thinking about adding an additional room to her house that she could rent.

Both women now sat at the table facing each other. Mary had requested tea and she was sipping it slowing. Sandra watched her carefully as she replaced the cup on the saucer.

"I want to make a proposal to you and I don't want you to answer until I am finished," Mary began.

"OK," Sandra replied, and nodded slowly.

Mary began to speak and when she finished Sandra was extremely confused and surprised. This white woman had just told her that she and her husband would legally adopt her child, once it turned out to be his. They were due to leave the island in about eighteen months to two years, at which time the child should be able to travel with them. Sandra could not believe her ears. She would not lose her job after all. Life would continue as usual, the only difference being that she was pregnant. She could continue to make plans to build that extra room, and maybe even an extra bathroom.

24

The daughter's experience

Sandra was seven months pregnant. The nausea had subsided but she was persistently tired. Mary would constantly fuss over her and she insisted that she visited the doctor every two weeks to make sure that the baby was well. For the past two months, Brendon had had little to do with her. He would always enquire about her health but there was no longer any intimacy. She knew that Mary had advised him not to have sex with her, in case it interfered with the progress of the baby. Mary also warned Sandra not to have sex, in case she damaged the baby. There was more to this than met the eye, however. Mary was growing jealous, because Brendon was now paying Sandra some attention. He would want to listen to the baby, and touch her stomach. Sandra could see the longing in his eyes each time he looked at her, especially now that her breasts were swollen with milk. He would come into the kitchen from time to time and beg her to let him suck them and she would oblige.

She was glad it was the summer holidays and that Maureen was helping her around the house. Today, Mary had gone to one of her group meetings. They were planning a fete to raise funds for orphaned children and she should have returned some time ago. Sandra was not too worried because she sometimes stayed longer with her friends and then Brendon would pick her up.

However, Brendon had just arrived home without Mary. Sandra asked where she was and he explained that one of her friends was bringing her home later. He said that he had had a hard day and was going to bed.

Sandra began to wonder where Maureen was and hoped that she would not disturb him. He said that after his rest he would give them both a lift home. When Brendon entered the bedroom, he noticed clothes on the bed. He knew immediately that they belonged to Maureen.

"Maureen," he called out. "I know you're in here. Just come out."

The wardrobe door opened slowly and Maureen stepped out. She was wearing one of Mary dresses.

"What the hell do you think you're doing?" He asked annoyed. "Take that dress off, RIGHT NOW!

He continued to look at her, as she stripped down to her bra and panties.

"I'm so..." He was seeing her near naked body for the first time. He noticed how mature it was. He felt the familiar tingling in his groin.

"Stop, stop," he told himself.

Maureen walked up to him touched him on the hand and looked at him with pleading eyes. "Please, don't tell."

He could not take his eyes off her chest. Her breasts were heaving. He could see that the brassiere was struggling to hold them in. His hands began to twitch.

I just want to touch them, they look so succulent, he thought.

Maureen was standing very close to him. He could smell her bodily scent. It smelt like acid. His nose burnt. They were eye to eye. Those eyes were glued on him. They were round, dark, and piercing. He felt hypnotised. He could feel his breath speeding up; he should not have had that final drink. He knew before he said yes to Sam his friend that he had had his quarto, but he couldn't ever turn him down. Sam had been the first local to make him feel welcome on the island and he continued to teach him how to survive. His head was spinning slightly.

Brendon couldn't believe what came out of his mouth next. "Take off the brassiere."

Maureen obeyed. She unhooked the strap and her breasts bounced out like two balloons happy to be released.

They're so big, so beautiful, he thought.

They were a lighter brown than the rest of her body. He pointed at them.

"Can I touch them?" He asked.

Maureen nodded. She had expected the person who had entered the room to be Mrs Payne. Her mother had warned her not to come into the master bedroom but she was bored, so, she took the opportunity to try on some of the lovely clothes in Mrs Payne's wardrobe. She was glad it was Brendon instead of his wife. They had always got on well, but she was frightened that he might tell his wife where he'd found her and what she was doing. She didn't want her mother to lose her job so she would do whatever he asked. She didn't want her mother to lose her job especially now that she was pregnant. So she nodded again.

When she spent time with her cousins, she had seen their boyfriends touching them this way. Many nights she had watched Mildred and George West in bed or, on the settee, when they thought she was asleep 'doing it'. He normally began with sucking her breast and Mildred would ask for more. She had wanted someone to touch her breasts for a long time. Brendon timidly touched the left one. She closed her eyes as she had seen Mildred do and pushed her breasts towards him.

"Ohhhh! How soft, how good they feel," he said as he now touched the right one.

He bent over and kissed the top of each one, just next to the nipples. He looked at Maureen face and noticed that her eyes were closed. She had pushed her chest towards him, but now she was motionless. He proceeded to kiss each nipple, one and then the other. Maureen gasped. He placed his head between her breasts and squeezed them together as if he was kneading bread. He found her mouth and kissed her full on the lips. He pushed his tongue into her mouth and forced her teeth apart. He pulled away and looked at her. Maureen's eyes were still closed and she was moving her tongue over her top and bottom lips as if to moisturise them.

"What succulent lips you have," he said.

He kissed her cheeks and her eyes.

There was still no movement from Maureen. Her eyes remained closed. He paused and looked over at the bed. His groin was on fire. His penis had been hardening for some time now. He had to relieve himself. Sandra had stopped having sex with him and Sally continued to be 'too tired'. He felt starved. He had to have this pretty thing. He lifted her up and placed her on the bed. He walked to the bedroom door and locked it.

Maureen lay motionless although she opened her eyes when she heard the door close. She immediately closed them again. She knew what was coming next. She had seen her cousins 'doing it'. They had played games. They would lie on each other, kiss, touch each other's private parts and move their hips. However, she knew that this would be different. From the first time he touched her it felt different. This was a man.

Her mother had warned her about men. She had told her that they could hurt you, but this was Mr Payne. She wouldn't mind. She knew that he would not hurt her. Brendon returned to the bed. He had taken off his clothes.

"Look at me," he ordered Maureen. "Open your eyes and look at me."

She opened her eyes and saw that Payne was completely naked. His arms and legs were tanned, however, the middle part of his body was very pale and his 'thing' was sticking out in front of him. Maureen looked at it curiously. There was some red straight hair around it. It looked like a pink stick stuck in the ground with red grass surrounding it. Maureen had never seen that colour hair before.

"Have you done this before?" he asked.

"Only playing with my cousins. That...that looks strange," she said pointing at his penis.

"Sit up," he ordered.

He pushed his hips towards her face and she sucked the penis deeper into her throat. She wanted to show him how good she could be. Suddenly he began to shake and Maureen felt her mouth filling up with liquid. "Swallow it," he demanded.

The liquid tasted like something she could not describe. He withdrew and his penis had creamy liquid dripping from its tip.

"Lick it off," Brendon ordered and pushed his penis at her once more.

"Good girl, good girl," he moaned.

"Lick around the tip. Place your tongue inside the tip," He instructed.

Oh my god! Oh my god!" Brendon moaned. Thank you. Thank you."

She released the penis which now lay limp in front of her.

He bent down and kissed her fill on the lips.

"Now lie still and I will tell you what to do. I'll not hurt you."

Payne knelt at the bottom of the bed at the foot of where Maureen lay. "Take off your panties." He began to kiss her toes on both feet, up between her legs and up to her thighs. When he reached her thighs, he spread her legs apart, licked his forefinger, and pushed it inside her vagina.

Maureen let out a hissing sound.

"Like that?" Brendon asked. "Nice and tight."

He pushed his finger in and out of her vagina.

Maureen was moving in time with his movements. She was making squealing sounds. He pushed his head between her legs and began to lick her inner thighs and then inside her vagina. Maureen squealed. The more he licked and sucked the higher the squeals became. He reached up and placed his hand on her mouth.

"Sssshhhh," he warned. "We don't want Sandra to hear. Feels good?" he asked. She nodded.

"Yes, do more, do more," she begged and thrust her hips towards his face. He smiled and looked at the clock on the dresser.

"Another time, perhaps. Put on your clothes, I have to take you and your mother home."

He kissed her full on the lips, looked at her and said.

"Don't tell anyone, this will be our secret."

He moved over to the dresser, took out a wad of notes, counted out ten and handed them to her. "Buy yourself something nice."

Two months later Sandra's second child was born.

Sandra nursed the baby for the first three months of its life while the adoption process was completed. When it was official six months later, Mary left the island and took the child with her.

Brendon stayed on to the end of the contract and he finally left eighteen months later.

Brendon wrote to both Sandra and Maureen. However, he hardly ever gave them news about the baby. She would love to know how 'young Brendon' as she had named him was getting on. His correspondence dried up after three years. Sandra wondered if Mary had stopped him writing to them.

25

Judge not

Good news travels fast; bad news travels even faster. The news of the Deacon's murder caused bedlam in Sally's village, in Sandra's village and the surrounding neighbourhoods. The Deacon was known for his charitable work and the fact that he had taken in a child when his mother died had endeared him to everyone. Shock and horror were expressed at this unfortunate deed. It was unimaginable that anyone could commit such a despicable act against such a good, godly man. Phones were ringing off the hook, as each of the callers tried to find out what had actually happened. Of course, everyone knew their truth. Everyone lamented his loss.

"Not our Deacon, he was such a good man and such a genius with the choir, too," one of those interviewed later by the radio station said.

“We certainly can’t replace him,” said another. These views were echoed around the community. The neighbours wanted to show their support for their Deacon and their contempt for the killer. Sally invited them to gather in her yard, and from there they marched to the local police station where the alleged killer was being interrogated. .

Sandra too, was listening to her radio that early morning and heard the sad news of the Deacon, and like everyone else had been shocked that someone would kill one of God’s chosen leaders. She shouted across to Maureen, who was busy preparing breakfast before leaving for work.

“He should burn in hell for that. Burn in hell.”

“Let’s wait to hear the circumstances, Mam,” Maureen replied.

She didn’t really care about what was happening in the news right now. She was angry with herself for never learning to drive and now that James had gone off to University in Trinidad, she would have to get the bus to work. She had taken a part-time job in the nursing home that Betty McClean had just opened. She wished she had not promised Betty that she would come in on a Saturday. There were only four residents, but Betty said that she expected a new patient today and wanted her to come in to help her settle the resident.

Maureen really wanted to stop working now that Trina had found a job as a secretary at the restaurant, and her relationship with Peter Preston, the owner, was progressing. It had developed much quicker than even she had anticipated. She was waiting to hear if he would agree to help her get an apartment.

She was, however, disappointed in Tracey, her other daughter. She had decided she wanted a child by the Indian salesman who was paying the rent for her one bedroom apartment.

“I want children with nice hair,” she told her mother, when she was trying to persuade her to have an abortion. “He wants this child, too.”

Maureen shook her head, because she knew better. She knew that men want children until they actually arrived, and then they disappeared. She didn’t think that this present situation with her daughter was going to be any different. She walked out of the house and onto the veranda, where her mother was sitting, reading the newspaper.

“I’m off. I should be back about three o’clock.”

“Mmmmm, enjoy” her mother replied. She didn’t look up from the paper. She had been reading the death notices. At seventy-five years, it was inevitable that she would find someone whom she knew. Sandra spent a lot of time on her veranda, with the phone next to her chair so that she could call when she needed to. When the one o'clock news came on and they announced that the person whom the police had originally arrested was being released and instead Martha's grandson, Teddy, was being charged with murder. She phoned Martha straight away.

She remembered Teddy's troubled childhood. He was never normal. When Martha explained what had happened between Teddy and the Deacon, Sandra promised to help should she need her to do so.

"Things are not always as they seem." She reminded herself.

She also recalled what Maureen had said to her earlier that morning. She knew what Maureen's first words would be when she got home from work that evening. By early afternoon; the group had grown so large that it would surround the police station. They had discussed breaking down the door because they wanted to get their hands on the boy who had dared to do such an unholy thing, but Sally and Lynn Reid had managed to stop that from happening. By the time Peter had finished in the garden, his yard was crowded, and half an hour later, they began to march to the police station

Sandra was lying across her bed after taking her afternoon nap when Maureen arrived about four o'clock. She rushed into mother's room.

"Hi, mam. Guess what?" She said, anticipation spread all over her face.

"No, don't tell me. I know I was wrong to judge," Sandra replied at once, waving her hands in the air.

"No, not that. Guess who the new patient is? Franklin Harris."

"Bless your heart and hope to die, don't lie to me." Sandra replied and sat up straight in the bed. She had an instant headache. She never thought she would hear the name of Thomas's father again, and now he was here, and his granddaughter was taking care of him. Maureen sat next to Sandra on the bed looked at her and continued more quietly.

"There's more, Mam. I met Thomas, my father."

Sandra said nothing, because, for one moment her mind went blank. Her heart jolted at the sound of his name. She pinched herself. "So, he turns up almost sixty years late." She looked at her daughter and tears began to run down her face.

"I'm sorry, Mam. I didn't mean to upset you."

"I'm not upset, dear. I was just remembering what could have been." She had lied and her daughter knew it. Maureen hugged her mother.

She knew what her mother had suffered over the loss of the only man she had loved. No one else had been able to take that place in her life. Joseph had come close, but even he failed. He had tried everything in his power to get her to marry him after his first wife had died, but Sandra was steadfast in her refusal. Her behaviour was strange. Those around her wondered if she was still waiting for Thomas to return.

“Tell me what happened.” Sandra said calmly.

26

Breaking the silence

Apart from Peter, the only other person who seemed unaffected and unperturbed by the death was Henry Preston, their son. He had not left the house. In fact, he had not even looked out at the crowd that had earlier occupied the yard.

When the news broke, Henry Preston was sitting at the dining table finishing his breakfast and his homework for the next school day. He always liked to do his homework at this time, because Sundays were taken up with activities associated with his church, and he was usually too tired at the end of the day. His mother, who was also in the dining room didn't notice his demeanour change after the radio announcement. She was consumed with the news. She ran to the door, where the neighbours were already gathering. Everything else was forgotten, including Henry.

He dropped his pen and began to tremble uncontrollably. Tears streamed down his face. His mouth was slightly open and the remnants of the bread he was chewing were visible. Crumbs began falling onto his chest and onto the table. Only six minutes had passed since the death announcement and Henry had been sitting in this position for about three of them.

Henry's brother, David hearing the commotion, rushed into the dining room to find out what was going on. He immediately noticed his brother's condition: Henry appeared stunned and disconcerted.

"What's the matter, Henry?" he asked, staring at his brother with concern etched all over his face. Henry responded by shaking his head. More crumbs fell from his slightly open mouth.

David was scared because Henry seemed incapable of doing anything. He fell forward and his head hit the table. His plate fell and the contents splattered over the floor.

"Mummy, Mummy, come in here, Henry's not well," David shouted anxiously through the door.

"What's wrong with him?"

She asked as she rushed into the house, leaving the group to continue their plans. She rushed to her son's side. She was a trained nurse and noticed instantly the need for urgent action.

"Help me lie him flat," she shouted to David. By now, Peter was standing at the doorway trying to keep some of the neighbours outside the house. He was pleading with them, "Please give Sally room to deal with Henry."

Sally quickly checked Henry's airway to ensure that he was able to breath and to remove anything that might cause a restriction.

"He's still breathing. Thank god," she exclaimed looking up at David.

"He seems to be in some kind of shock. Call an ambulance."

On Monday, the call came from one of Maureen's taxi-driver friends that there was a white man from England who was asking if they knew her or her mother. The man was staying at Roserock Hotel and had given him his contact details so that they could get in touch with him at once. Both Sandra and Maureen knew immediately who the white man was. Sandra wondered why he was back. She thought about the son she had borne them, and hoped that he had done well. Over the years she had thought about him. She often wondered what he looked like and whether he was married. Sandra remained grateful for the money Mary and Brendon had given her, because it had had allowed her to add an apartment to the house.

Sandra and Maureen arranged to meet with Brendon at his hotel and he sent a taxi to pick them up the Tuesday morning. Brendon was struck by how well his dark-skinned lovers looked, even now in Sandra was in her twilight years. He had never forgotten them, their passion and sensitivity. Making love to his wife was never the same afterwards. The fervour was not there. When she died he had wanted to leave England, return this place and marry one or the other. However, he had a son to bring up. Brendon wanted to provide him with the best opportunities for his educational advancement.

The priesthood was the last thing Brendon had wanted for his son, but that was his choice. He had left England some years ago and had worked in Africa, South America before ending up in the Caribbean. All his correspondence spoke about his love of the people he worked with. Now he was dead, murdered, and he was here to find out what had happened.

He was not here, therefore, to reclaim the two beautiful and now mature women who sat across the table from him. He had, instead, to inform them that the Deacon who was murdered was their son and brother.

They engaged in small talk as they ate breakfast. Then Brendon paused and cleared his throat because he knew that it was time to give them the unfortunate news. He waited for the maid to clear the table. He asked the server to bring him a copy of the day's newspaper. He had already seen the front page, but in order to give them the information, he needed them to see the front part.

He held it up in front of him. The headlines read, *"Community in shock over Deacon's death. Police still investigating!"*

A picture of the Deacon in his church regalia accompanied the headline.

"Yes," they both said in unison and looked at him.

"Well! Don't you recognize him?"

"No, I don't."

"He's your son."

"Who? No, he can't be." Sandra now screamed. "No child of mine could have done what he did."

"Sssssssshhhhh, Mam. Everyone is watching."

"What did he do?" Brendon asked, surprised.

"Let's go somewhere more private. Let's go to my room."

Sandra's head was getting hot and it was spinning fast. She heard someone shout, "She's falling." The next thing she knew was that she was laying on her back on the floor. Maureen was standing over her with a concerned look on her face. She could hear Brendon's voice in the background repeatedly saying, "I really didn't mean to upset her, but I thought that she needed to know."

Someone replied.

"Please Sir, just step aside, we will deal with this. She's really going to be fine."

Someone shone a light in her eyes and a male voice asked her name and if she knew where she was. She couldn't remember the name of the hotel but answered the other questions correctly.

Maureen was advised to take Sandra to her doctor straight away for a full check up, just in case she had suffered a stroke. Brendon paid the taxi to take them to the doctor and then home. He apologized again and said that he was going to be in the country for a month and would keep in touch.

Back at the house, Maureen had a hard time persuading her mother to go to bed. She felt energized and wanted to phone Martha to tell her the latest news. Later that night she went into her mother's room and lay down next to her on the bed. Her mother turned to her and said. "I can't believe that I gave birth to a monster like that."

"But, Mam," she replied earnestly. "You didn't raise him. Remember he was adopted."

"But what could have turned him into such a monster?"

Maureen shrugged her shoulders but didn't say anything. She remained quiet because she was thinking about Brendon. Maureen had never had the courage to tell her mother what happened between them. She had arranged to meet him at the hotel that evening after making sure that Sandra was well enough to be left alone.

"Now about this father of yours: are you going to see him again?" Sandra asked breaking the silence.

"Well, so long as I continue to work, there's no doubt that I will see him. Remember he only sired me. You were the one who made me who I am. However, would you want to see him?"

"I don't know. I really don't know. He was from another life."

27

Let the truth prevail

Henry lay quietly, feeling pensive. It had been two days since he had been discharged from the hospital. His mother and father were sitting either side of his bed looking at him anxiously. Since he regained consciousness, every family member wanted to know what had happened. No one had asked him outright, but the questions were evident on their faces. However, his mind was still in turmoil. He remained quiet except for asking one question.

"Is the Deacon really dead?"

Whenever he got the answer, he would look straight ahead; his eyes would glaze, as if he wanted to cry, but instead he would tremble uncontrollably.

The doctor who treated Henry told his parents that he was in emotional shock. The problem appeared to be psychological, so he advised that Henry should see a specialist. His parents were reluctant to do this. His mother, in particular, felt that they could handle whatever problems Henry was going through at home. She lamented, “These doctors are too quick to diagnose, and lock away.”

Apart from this, she didn’t want her friends and neighbours to know that a member of the family had ‘those type’ of problems.

Peter disagreed. He felt that some kind of help was needed for his son. He hoped that the school guidance counsellor could speak to him. He had noticed that recently Henry had not been looking his usual boisterous self. Instead, he was looking anxious and depressed. Peter wished he could spend more time with his children. However, the business and now Trina, kept him very busy. He began to consider changing his schedule so that he could get home earlier when they were still awake.

The doctor recommended that Henry should take part in activities to keep his keep his mind off the incident and that he should be allowed to have all his favourite things, or pets, around him.

Sally was unwilling to have the dog, Pip, in the house, because she felt that dogs belong in the yard and not in the house. He would only bring in germs. She therefore had him tied up a way from the house as otherwise he would sit outside Henry's bedroom window whining and scratching on the sideboards of the house.

Peter knew that there was no point arguing with her about this decision. So he bought a television for Henry's bedroom and David brought in all his martial arts videos for him to watch.

For the first two days Henry would stare blankly at the television screen or he would sleep. Later, however, he began mimicking the actors' actions on the screen, repeating the phrases they used, and moving his arms and legs as they did when they were fighting.

One day, however, he seemed to have regressed. When his mother woke him he asked her the one question that everyone hoped they would never hear asked again. Instead of replying, his mothers asked him to take a shower, put on some clothes and join the others at breakfast. He replied with a firm, "NO "then curled up in the foetal position on the bed.

That was two hours ago and since then every member of the immediate family had tried to coax him out of bed but to no avail.

Peter knew exactly what he needed to do. He got up and returned with Pip who barked with joy when he saw his master and immediately Henry sat up straight in bed. The dog jumped up and began licking Henry's face, his hair and his neck. Both seemed equally excited to see each other. Those watching were amazed at what they were witnessing, except for Sally. She was screaming at the top of her voice.

"That dog is dirty. He's bringing germs into my house. Eyuk! Eyuk!"

"Oh, shut up," Peter said looking at her irritably. He pointed at the scene on the bed.

"Can't you see what's happening there?"

She looked and saw her son, who minutes previously had been refusing to even turn to face them, jumping up and down on the bed with his dog and smiling widely. They were face-to-face, nose-to-nose and purr to hand.

Sally got up slowly from the chair in the bedroom, where she had sat before the commotion began, turned towards the door, opened it and slammed it behind her. She shuddered against the closed door. She could not bear the sight of her son kissing and cuddling with a dog, and certainly not on the clean sheets – she had only put them on the bed the day before. She returned to the room a few minutes later armed with a clean set of sheets, an aerosol of disinfectant spray and a clean pair of pyjamas for Henry.

However, the scene that greeted her return was much more tranquil than when she left the room. The dog was lying on the bed with his head on Henry's lap. Henry was looking down and patting him on the head, with a wide grin on his face; his thoughts still appeared to be far away.

The dog was wagging his tail ever so slightly. They both looked contented.

Henry was thirteen years old and scared. Today he felt much older. He wanted to block from his thoughts what he seen and heard. He looked around at his family in turn and wondered what he could say to them that would not get him into trouble. Both parents sitting at the bottom of his bed and asking him what had happened that had made him so sick the day, the... They were all trying so hard not to say that name. However, he wanted to know if it was true.

"Did he really die?" Henry asked again.

This time when he said it to his mother, she didn't insist on him having a bath. However, he had to know for sure, before he could speak. He was angry with them, all of them, because they refused to tell him the truth. Then his father had brought Pip in and he felt much better. Pip had been his only friend, the only one he was able to tell the truth. Then, his Father had shouted at his Mother to shut up. He had never known him to get that angry with her before and he knew that it was all his fault. He wanted so badly to tell them what had happened, but what if they didn't believe him? He yawned.

After all the excitement with Pip, who was now lying at the bottom of his bed, he was beginning to feel tired again. He was not ready to speak, not yet. He had to be certain that the Deacon was dead.

His father was the last to leave, but just before he left he whispered, just before he closed the bedroom door, "Yes, Henry, the Deacon is really dead."

They left him alone to get some sleep, but sleep would not come. There was too much on his mind.

Henry had destroyed a letter his teacher had given to him for his parents the previous Friday. He had opened it. It mentioned that 'in the past three months Henry had been displaying low self-esteem, was found crying in the bathroom and had also become very hostile towards other students. As a result, his grades had fallen drastically'. He couldn't tell them he had destroyed the letter. Worst of all he couldn't tell them what had happened with the Deacon. The fact that he was now dead and in heaven, at the right hand of God would make it more certain that the Deacon from his lofty position would make sure he burnt in hell.

He visualized the Deacon in heaven; all decked out in a white robe, together with his halo and wings. On the other hand, he imagined Simon in hell stoking the fire for the devil. There were horns growing out of Simon's head. He was all hot and sweaty and grinning wildly and vigorously as he stoked the fire.

Henry shivered.

Simon's not dead, he reminded himself. He wondered how Simon was faring at the police station. Maybe they were beating him so that he would confess.

Had they released him? He wondered.

He was certain that Simon knew what the Deacon had done, because of the last encounter he had had with him. Maybe Simon had told the police what he had seen between him and the Deacon and now they would be coming for him.

Maybe Simon too, had the same experience with the Deacon, Henry thought.

That could explain the reason for that vicious attack. He could have been jealous.

If they released him, he could be coming after me to kill me, too.

The same anxiety that he felt when he heard about the death seized him again. He began to shake and sweat. He bent over and cuddled his dog.

28

The confrontation

The Friday, before the death, Simon had confronted Henry on the Deacon's veranda. He wanted to know what the Deacon did when they went into the bedroom; Henry had not replied because he was terrified of the consequences. Apart from that he was embarrassed that someone else would know what the Deacon had done. He was uncomfortable and dropped his head whilst trying to rush passed Simon without replying. Simon had grabbed him roughly by his right arm as he tried to get by him, and hissed crossly in his ear.

"I want to know what he did. Did he touch you?" Henry grew more frightened and tried to pull away from him.

"Let me go! Let me go!" He screamed at Simon and continued to pull away.

There was a loud thud as the books he held fell on the veranda's wooden floor. The Deacon heard the noise and rushed to the door.

"What's going on out there?" He asked.

Simon hurriedly let go of Henry's arm. He looked at the Deacon with disgust. The Deacon looked at both Simon and Henry in turn. No one spoke. They were both looking at the Deacon for instructions.

"Simon, I believe you have some chores to do inside the house," he said looking angrily at Simon.

Simon knew from his tone and the, 'I'll deal with you later' look, that he was dismissed. With one last sideways glance at Henry, Simon pushed passed the Deacon and went into the house. The Deacon bent down and picked up Henry's books and handed them to him. He touched Henry gently on his shoulder and his voice softened as he said,

"You go home now, Henry."

Henry was close to tears and was glad to be allowed to leave. Henry was halfway home, when he realized that he had left his school bag in the Deacon's living room. He had been in such a hurry to leave the house after the incident in the bedroom that he had only picked up the two books that the Deacon had given him to read. He had placed them on the table in the hallway so that he would not forget them. He turned around straight away. He needed his bag in order to complete his homework for Monday. Now was the best time to fetch it, because he knew someone else was in the house. The Deacon only took him to his bedroom when there was no one else at home.

As he neared the Deacon's house, Henry could hear the sound of piano music. It became louder as he approached the road leading to the house. Then it suddenly stopped. He quietly opened the gate and walked up the pathway towards the steps and onto the veranda. He could hear angry raised voices coming from inside. One was quieter than the other: he recognized it as the Deacon. He sounded as if he was trying to calm down the other person. The other voice was definitely a man. Henry assumed it was Simon.

Henry instantly became fearful. He hated arguments and this one sounded like a bad one. His fear grew when he heard Simon in an irate voice shouting,

"It has to stop, and stop NOW! No more. You are BAD, BAD!"

The Deacon was pleading with him.

"No! No! Please don't. Please. Please, I beg you. Let's talk."

There was a pause and the Deacon screamed "SIMON!"

His voice became muffled and he let out a gurgling sound. From his vantage point at the bottom of the steps, Henry couldn't see anything, but his instinct told him that he should leave the school bag. He could only imagine that Simon had done something dreadful to the Deacon. Whatever was going on in that house he certainly didn't want to be a part of it.

When Henry arrived home, he ran straight to his room. He was trembling hysterically. He began to cry quietly. What could he do? Whom could he tell? Who would believe him? The Deacon had said that he was anointed and if Henry told anyone what was happening between them then Henry would go to hell. Henry wished he had the courage to run away from home.

The Deacon was a close family friend and a mentor to all in the district and beyond. His mother believed in him. Henry had begun going to his house to practise the piano because his piano teacher had left the district. The Deacon had persuaded his mother to let him use his piano to practise whilst she looked for another music teacher. That was six months ago and the Deacon had now become his unofficial piano teacher. His mother was very pleased that he was prepared to make that kind of sacrifice. How could he tell her he didn't want to go to his house anymore? His mother would be disappointed because she was relying on him to become the musician in the family since David had given up the violin.

The Deacon had touched him there. No one

had ever done that except his mother when she was explaining how to pull back the skin to clean himself both inside and out. He had kissed it. He made Henry touch his. He said it made him feel good. The Deacon had hurt him and when he cried, he told him he would soon get accustomed to it. He explained that Henry's parents understood what he was doing, because they too would have gone through the same initiation when they were his age. He said that if what he was doing was revealed, his mother, in particular, would be very upset. The Deacon made him promise on *The Bible* to keep their relationship secret. He said that what they did was sacred and should never be divulged. He said that they had a special relationship.

There were two things that Henry was terrified of: going to hell, and upsetting his mother. Now the Deacon was dead and Simon had been arrested. No one knew, yet, that Henry had heard the altercation between Simon and the Deacon. No one, except perhaps for the Deacon, who heard the last words Simon hissed at Henry on the veranda that evening as he disappeared inside the house. "This must stop now."

He began to shiver and shake once more. He held Pip even closer to him in the bed. He was scared, very scared, but believed that it was time he spoke to his father.

Peter Preston had also decided that it was

time to speak to his son, to ask him those troubling questions he had been repeating to himself, but not getting the type of answers that made any sense to him. He pushed opened the bedroom door, almost knocking Henry and the dog over. They were on their way out of the room.

"Sorry, Henry, I was coming to speak to you." Peter said.

He noticed that Henry was looking very sad. His eyes were red and his father suspected that he must have been crying as he was still sniffling.

"I was coming to find you, too," Henry responded. His father closed the door, held Henry by the shoulders, and asked.

"Are you alright? I have been worried about you."

An hour later Sally knocked, pushed opened the door and began speaking simultaneously.

"Peter, Teddy was arrested for murdering the D..." She stopped dead in her tracks, the doorknob was still held in her hand. She looked at both her husband and son, and felt the sadness permeating the room. Henry was crying and Peter held closely and whispered to him softly.

"You cry dear, everything will be taken care off. He'll never hurt you again."

Peter's back had been to the door but as he turned around to face Sally she noticed that he too had tears in his eyes and that they were falling freely down his cheeks.

"What's going on? What happened? Who will not hurt Henry again?"

She stepped inside the room and shut the door abruptly and loudly.

By the following Monday evening, the story of the Deacon had broken. A different kind of shock pervaded the small community of St Jude's after the news spread that the Deacon had 'molested' boys for whom he was providing pastoral care. A mass despondency fell upon the community. Families gathered to discuss their relationship with him. His status went from adulation and hero worship to utter contempt and loathing.

It seemed that he had had his way with many of the young men in the district. Men and boys now came forward and told their own stories about their encounters with the Deacon. Parents who had dismissed their children's complaints as youthful imagination wrung their hands in shame. "If only... If only...," one of the mothers desolately announced.

She was abruptly interrupted and gently reminded that, "Hindsight is twenty-twenty vision."

Some parents who had suspected, but kept their thoughts to themselves having withdrawn their children from the Deacon's presence, now came forward. Those who recalled that at one time or other, their children had visited his house to seek counsel, were now quizzing the young men and boys, in particular.

"Did he touch you, too?"

They were questioned. Professional eyes searched their faces for the unspoken answers.

Questions were posed to the church leaders who descended on the village.

"Why did you send him here?" "Who can we now trust?" "Who will now look after our spiritual and emotional guidance?"

29

The end of an affair

Peter had not seen Trina since the Friday before the death of the Deacon. They had spent the evening together at the apartment she now shared with a friend, for which Peter was paying the rent. She had been calling him on his cell phone, but he had turned it off.

Tuesday was his first day back and he was not intending to stay the whole day. His assistant could take over for the next few weeks, while he made plans with his family to take a holiday.

Trina stormed into his office excitement etched all over her face.

"I've been phoning you. Why the fuck didn't you answer?"

She leaned over his desk to kiss him. Peter pulled away. He was somewhat taken aback by the profanity. He had been trying for some time to get her to stop swearing, especially at work. She ignored him, and continued to speak.

"What about the murder? Did you hear about it?"

She babbled. She jumped off the desk, and came around to his side and sat on his lap.

"Guess what?"

She got up and walked around his desk again.

"What?"

Peter replied as he rearranged the papers on his desk. She was irritating him. He wanted her to leave so he could clear his desk in an effort to avoid Denzil needing to contact him when he took his break. However, the next statement she made caused his blood pressure to go up, he was certain, by one hundred per cent.

"The Deacon? He's my uncle," she smirked.

"What do you mean?" he asked seeking clarification. After he heard the story about her grandmother, Sandra and the relationship with Brendon and the birth of a son, he began to wonder what he was doing spending time with someone like Trina. He began to look at her in a very different light.

She was very animated as she told him the sordid details of her grandmother's arrangement with an English couple. She stood in front of him and danced around like a gazelle on heat joyfully relating her meeting with her grandmother and her mother's relationship with the English man. She obviously saw nothing wrong with this arrangement, but it made Peter feel sick inside. He wanted to vomit.

She wouldn't know what her 'uncle' has done to his son but he still wanted to tell her to shut up. He wanted to tell her to get out. There were so many hurtful things he wanted to say to her, but he didn't, because it was not her fault. None of this was her fault. She was simply playing the role that she had been well trained for.

When Trina was ready to leave for the day, she asked if he wanted to come by later. He told her he was not sure as he had to deal with family matters.

Peter had had a rough morning. He just could not settle. He had planned to finish his handover information by lunchtime and was still at the office at 4pm. He didn't complete all the things he wanted to before leaving the office. He handed over to Denzil anyway knowing that he was capable of dealing with those things that were outstanding. Denzil also knew how to contact him should he need any help. Peter went straight to his son's room when he arrived home. Henry was fast asleep and Sally was fast asleep on the chair next to his bed. She stirred when he entered the room.

Good, he thought.

Aloud he said to his wife. “How was he today?”

“OK,” she whispered. “This is tiring though.”

He shook his head and thought. *So was working for that monster, I’m sure*.

He was still angry with her although she was happy to let him take charge. He would make all the plans for what the family would now do.

He closed the door quietly and went to bathe. He planned to see Trina later, to offer her an explanation about what he was about to do. Sally looked at his back as he left the room. She could not understand why he was treating her in this off-hand matter. She knew that she had made a terrible mistake and was sorry. She had been trying for the past few days to make up for the error, but he continued to ignore her efforts.

She was floored when she heard what had happened to her son and had declared furiously.

“I worked with him! We spent hours together seeking out those in need. I don’t understand. I, I, can’t. I can’t.” She had broken down and wept.

She looked at her husband and screamed at him. “FOR CHRIST’S SAKE! HE WAS OUR SPIRITUAL LEADER!”

Then calming slightly, “My, my own son! So help me God, if he wasn’t dead already I would kill him myself,” she then screamed angrily.

“My sentiments exactly, Peter had replied. “I feel nothing but utter contempt for that man.”

Yet, Sandra still felt that Peter paid no attention to anything she had to say. She wanted to tell him that the Deacon's father was on the island. However, he bathed, ate and left the house again without even saying where he was going.

Peter turned the corner into the street adjoining Trina's apartment. He parked as he usually did and walked the hundred yards to the apartment. The building was a block of eight identical apartments on two levels. Her apartment was one of the corner ones on the ground floor. Outside he noticed a woman embracing a man. He could only see the woman's back but he had no doubt that it was Trina. No one could mistake that figure. The man placed his hands on her buttocks and pressed her close. She giggled and pecked him on the cheek. She gripped him by the hand and was about to lead him into the apartment, when she turned and she saw Peter approaching.

Uh! Peter, I didn't expect you," she announced surprised.

She dropped the man's arm straight away. The man, seeing Peter's fury, backed away from the door and down the driveway leading to the street. Not once did he take his eyes off Peter. The man kept repeating with his hands raised apologetically.

"I don't want any trouble, Mister, I didn't know..." He finally made it to his car, got in and roared away down the street.

Trina stood at the door defiantly, hands on hips. “What do you expect? I’m not your wife. You don’t own…”

Before she could finish the sentence Peter had pushed her hard in the chest with the palm of the hand. She stumbled back into the living room of the apartment and fell on the settee. Peter followed her. He grabbed her by the arm and pulled her protesting into the bedroom, before pushing her down onto the bed. She continued to protest, she continued to fight, she continued to resist, but it was to no avail. He ripped off her thin cotton dress and took her in a way he had never done before.

Trina was snoring hard next to him. He could see the bruises on her body from the initial struggle. Her fighting spirit had turned to fear and she had given in to his violence. He was sorry that he had taken her that way and he had said so afterwards. However, she simply nodded and said nothing; he could still see the fear in her eyes.

Peter continued to look at her. He knew he had to go; it was almost twelve and he needed to discuss the plans he had made with the other family member. Most of all he wanted to speak to Henry. He kissed Trina on her cheek and quietly left the apartment.

30

Inducement

After they released Simon he walked to the place he had always loved. This was somewhere that his mother used to bring him together with his siblings to picnic. He sat facing the sea on one of the benches and watched the ebb and flow of the mid-day tide. His mind went back to the incidents of the previous day. Everything was very confused. What had begun as a nice day had deteriorated into what he now thought to be the second worse day of his life.

He pondered this and wondered what his next move should be. He was fifteen years old and had nowhere to go. He had nowhere to live. He had no family and no friends. He was considering going back to the Deacon's house and sleeping in the shed that night until he saw a woman approaching him. She had been walking very slowly up the hill and he recognized her as the person who had been at the station earlier that morning with Teddy Clarke.

"Hello," she said.

She was breathing heavily. Martha Clarke sat on the bench next to him. She had intended to speak to him at the station, but by the time she came outside, he had already disappeared. Initially they were both quiet but then Martha spoke.

Loud snoring coming from the bedroom that used to be Teddy's woke Martha. When she went to investigate Teddy was fast asleep on the bed. His clothes were covered in blood. She called the police. She watched from the doorway as the police questioned Teddy about the blood on his clothes. He simply kept repeating that he had saved Simon from the Deacon, and that "the Deacon was a bad man.

"He's bad. He hurt me," he repeated.

Martha told Simon that she blamed herself for what had happened to Teddy. Lucy, her daughter, had abandoned Teddy at the hospital, when she found out that he would never be a normal child and Martha had taken responsibility for raising him.

Teddy had been fourteen when the Deacon first came to live in the village. Martha had asked him if he had any odd jobs around the house that Teddy could do. Martha had been grateful to him for his help with Teddy. One day whilst she had been cleaning Teddy's room, she found some pornographic magazines. When she questioned him about them, Teddy screamed at her.

"Tell the Deacon, tell the Deacon to stop. He hurt me, bad, bad."

She could not get him to explain any more, and since she didn't understand what he meant, she discussed it with the Deacon. He said he didn't know what he meant either, but that he would speak to Teddy. He added, however, that he too was becoming worried about Teddy's behaviour of late. He explained that Teddy was sometimes physically abusive with the younger children, and he was worried that this might lead to other types of abuse. He suggested that they needed to save Teddy from himself before this happened. He recommended the hospital for mental retardation at the other side of the country. On his recommendation, Teddy was placed in a Mental Institute. That had been two years ago.

Teddy had escaped on the day of the murder and had headed straight to the Deacon's house. He was still obsessed with the Deacon, and his constant refrain remained, "He hurt me, bad." Martha had visited him a week ago and as usual he had begged her to take him home.

Simon listened to Martha but remained quiet.

He continued to look out at the horizon. Silence fell between them again. Martha looked at him and noticed that he was close to tears. He let out a loud sob. Martha spoke again.

"I used to love coming up here when I was a child with my best friend Sandra and watching the young and not so young, men dive off the stones, over there."

She pointed to the south of where they were sitting. He turned to look in the same direction. She too had tears in her eyes.

"Well," she continued and looked at him. "What are you going to do now?"

He shook his head but said nothing.

"The only way I could make up for what has happened to you is to offer you somewhere to live," she announced hesitantly, "that is, if you want to."

Martha didn't wait for him to reply but continued, "You can spend the night and then decide in the morning what you wish to do, but for now let's go and find you some food."

Simon didn't reply but hugged her tightly. She got up off the bench and reached out her hand. Simon looked at it suspiciously but then took it. They walked down the slope slowly.

"I'm so sorry," she said, remorsefully.

By now, they were in her kitchen and Simon had finished the plate of food that Martha had placed in front of him.

Apart from 'Yes', 'No', and 'Thank you' he had hardly spoken.

That night he went to bed much happier than he had been in a long time.

"Wolf in sheep's clothing is the only way he that man could be described."

Martha concluded. Like the others, who had so much faith in the Deacon she had chosen to dismiss Teddy's complaints as fantasies.

"He was a wicked man who took advantage of a boy who had nowhere to go," Martha stated looking at Sandra, anger evident on her face.

They had met at their usual spot at their usual time. That is, twice a month on the ridge overlooking their beloved 'Strip' to catch up on local and international gossip.

Sandra shook her head from to time as Martha continued to explain what Simon had told her about his life with the Deacon.

He had explained to her that one day; he had left work early because there was an electrical outage. He would normally attend his evening classes in motor vehicle engineering at the local college, but those were also cancelled, because the instructor was ill.

As he approached the Deacon's house he heard the sound of someone practicing the piano. It was a Friday and he surmised that it must be Henry. He normally came straight from school every Friday to get lessons.

He walked quietly up the steps to the veranda and sat on the chair to listen to the music. The playing stopped.

He's not bad, he thought, nodding his head in approval.

The louvres were open slightly, and through them, he could see the Deacon, Mr Payne, sitting to the left of Henry on the stool. He had his arm round him and he was speaking quietly. The Deacon appeared to be rubbing and massaging Henry's shoulders with his left hand as he spoke. He removed his hand from Henry's shoulder and placed it on Henry's lap. He continued to speak to Henry and they both got up. The Deacon held Henry's hand and led him towards the bedroom.

He began to shiver. *No! no!* He said to himself. *I don't believe it, not him too*.

He got up as quietly as he could and crept down the stairs. He walked back in the direction he had come. He would wait for another ten minutes, before approaching the house again.

Thus, returning at a later time that was closer to his regular time for coming home. He didn't want the Deacon to know what he had witnessed; he surprised himself by realizing that he was jealous.

He thought about himself and how the Deacon had initiated him. He had not wanted to do what the Deacon requested, but had no choice.

Now he had become accustomed to it and there were nights when he actually wanted the Deacon to call him to his bedroom. The Deacon could at times be cruel, but he is the only family he knew. Now though it seemed that he was to be replaced. There was someone else taking his place and he didn't like it.

Henry was the same age as he had been when he came to live with the Deacon – the relationship had began almost immediately. He wondered how far things had gone with Henry.

Was this the first time? He asked himself.

He shuddered. If it was he understood what Henry would be going through. He was ambivalent. On the one hand, he was frightened and sad for Henry; on the other he was envious, because he didn't want to be usurped. He now remembered two other students who abruptly stopped coming to the house to practise the piano. When he had asked the Deacon about them, he had been told that their parents no longer lived in the area. He now wondered if the Deacon had tried to seduce them also. Whatever the circumstances he would do what he had to do ensure it didn't continue.

As planned, Simon returned to the house ten minutes later and Henry was leaving. Simon saw him coming from the bedroom fixing his trousers. Simon waited outside on the veranda for him; he knew that he had to put a stop to what was happening between Henry and the Deacon. He had not yet worked out how, but he had to stop another child from suffering as he had done.

Simon had lost his mother when he was twelve years old years old. She had been brutally murdered, and Simon had found her body in a pool of blood. He was found lying next to her body having cried himself to sleep. His other three siblings were sent to live with relatives, but no one wanted him.

The Deacon immediately took him under his wing and later adopted him. The whole village thought this was a benevolent act. No one knew what was secretly going on inside the house. No one knew about the verbal, physical, and sexual assaults.

Simon had been accustomed to corporal punishment, because his mother had never 'spared the rod'. She had a special piece of electrical cord that she would use to beat the children. When the cord was out of reach she used whatever was within her grasp. She was a big woman and she could come at you close fisted or with her palm opened. Her hands worked like lightning on any part of your body she deemed suitable. He recalled the pot of hot soup that had been thrown in his direction because he had nodded his head instead of saying 'yes' to her. It didn't matter that that night they all went to bed hungry. Her boyfriends took their cue from her and would also beat the children mercilessly.

Six months after he had moved in with the Deacon, he was summoned into his bedroom for the first time. The Deacon explained that he had a pain at the back of his neck and asked Simon to rub some cream on the area to relieve the pain. Simon knelt on the bed behind the Deacon to apply the lotion.

"Mmmmmmmmmm. That feels very good, Simon. You have very gentle hands. You can stop now."

As Simon stepped off the bed, the Deacon said. "Close the jar and give it to me."

Simon passed the jar to him, and turned to leave the room.

"Come here, Simon."

Simon walked back and stood in front of him.

"Thank you for helping me. Come; let me give you a hug."

He hugged him tightly.

"We must look out for each other and help each other," he whispered in his ear.

"You and me, we're family now." He kissed Simon on his neck. "Now go and finish washing up the dishes."

He slapped him lightly on his buttocks as he walked away. "Don't forget to bring me my nightcap."

"OK, Sir," Simon replied and left the room.

Simon knew that Ms Drakes, the housekeeper, would normally leave the flask with the Deacon's night cap in the kitchen. When Simon returned to the Deacon's bedroom with the flask, he was already in bed. He handed Simon a key, pointed to the safe in the corner of the room, and said, "Open the safe over there. Take out one of the bottles of rum and bring it to me."

The Deacon took the bottle from Simon. He opened it and poured some of its contents into the cup of cocoa which he had already poured from the flask.

"Now, this is our secret, Ms Drakes is not to know about this. When I have finished, I want you to wash the cup. Do you want some of the cocoa? Go and get a cup and have some."

"Join me," he said and patted the side of the bed.

They sat next to each other on the bed and drank the cocoa laced with rum. The Deacon continued to speak as they drank, and from time to time, he would touch Simon, on his shoulder, on his leg, his head. He spoke about the fun they would have living together and the secrets they would share. He stressed that this was the first of them. Simon felt happy for the first time since coming to live in the house. He had missed his mother and siblings because he had not yet established contact with them. He had written to his Aunt, asking how they were, and if he could visit, but had not heard anything from her. He was not sure if the Deacon liked him, but was grateful to have a roof over his head, especially as his relatives had not wanted him.

Simon's father had disappeared long before he was born, and his mother had never spoken about him. When her Aunt had informed Simon that he was to live with the Deacon, he had begun to cry. However, she had said that he was a good man and that he would be fine. Everyone else confirmed this. Everything was turning out exactly as they had said, and he was happy that he was the one chosen to live with the Deacon.

31

The unnatural act

For the next seven nights, the Deacon shared his nightcap with Simon after he had rubbed him down with lotion. They were both very happy. On the eighth night when Simon entered the room he realized that the Deacon was in the shower. He turned back and was about the leave.

“No! no! Don’t leave,” the Deacon called. Simon hesitated. “Come in I want you to rub my back.”

Simon moved towards the shower.

“No, not dressed. Take off your clothes. You can’t do that with your clothes on. Come on! Come on, hurry up, the water is wasting,” He said impatiently.

Simon took off his clothes slowly. He stepped into the shower behind the Deacon who had soaped the flannel that he now passed it to him.

"Here, rub from my neck down."

Simon began gingerly; water was splashing from the Deacon's shoulder into his eyes. This made it difficult for him as he was constantly squinting and moving his head from side to side to avoid the splashing water.

"Come on; come on, rub harder than that." The Deacon was becoming irritated. Simon though tall for his age was having trouble reaching the Deacon's neck.

"I can't reach so high up." Henry said in a timid voice as he once again attempted to stretch up to his neck.

"Just do where you can," the Deacon replied. "Right that feels good, very good."

The Deacon continued to wash the front area of his body, whilst Simon continued to wash his back for a few minutes more. Suddenly the reached down and turned up the shower. He turned to face Simon.

"Now let me have the flannel. I will rub you." He took the flannel from Simon and began to rub the soap on it. Simon had not moved.

"Come on the inside." The Deacon said hurriedly.

Simon reluctantly moved to the inside of the shower facing the showerhead. The Deacon began to soap him and to rub him with the flannel. He began on his neck, his back working his way down to his buttocks and down to his legs.

"Turn around," he said but Simon hesitated.

The Deacon sucked his teeth, held him by the shoulder, and turned him around. Simon turned and noticed that the Deacon's penis was erect. Simon could not take his eyes away.

"What are you looking at?" the Deacon asked and he too looked down. "Oh that! Would you like to touch it?"

"No, Sir" Simon said and shook his head. "It would be wrong," he said hesitantly.

"I want you to," the Deacon said sternly. "Touch it. Come on."

The Deacon reached for Simon's hand and placed it once again on his penis, and placed his own hands over Simon's. "Keep it there," he insisted.

Simon knew he had no choice. He dropped his head to the floor of the shower. He felt the penis vibrate under his touch. Then his hand fell off.

The Deacon raised Simon's chin and forced him to look up at him.

"That felt very good." His voice had changed. It had gone into a higher pitch. "We are family now, remember," he continued sternly.

He held Simon head in such a position that he was looking directly at his erection.

"We have nothing to hide from each other. Understand!" Simon didn't answer, but attempted to nod his head. "I can't hear you." This time there was anger in his voice.

"Yes, Sir," Simon responded nervously.

He didn't know what it all meant but remained quite still as the Deacon continued to wash his body. He rubbed his head, his shoulders, and moved down to his chest and continued down to his legs and between his legs, and down to his feet. Simon felt strange to have another adult bathe him. His mother had stopped bathing him when he was six years old. However, the Deacon was very gentle as he washed him all over. He lingered extra long when he got to his penis.

"Can I touch yours?" the Deacon asked.

Simon said nothing. There were tears in his eyes. What could he say? What could he do? The Deacon continued to plead.

"I asked you a question. Can I touch yours? I want you to say yes. You have to be willing. It will be our secret. No one will ever know. Think of the fun we can have. You had fun this week, didn't you? I want you to say yes. Say yes, touch me."

Tears streamed down Simon's face as he nodded. "Yes. Touch me."

The Deacon knelt and gently touched Simon's penis. He massaged it, and it began to stiffen.

"Ouch!" Simon said. He was looking straight ahead of him. He could not look at what the Deacon was doing. The Deacon continued to massage his penis. Simon shivered in pain.

“Remember, what happens in this house is between you and me. We are a family now, and what happens in here remains in here.

“Yes, Sir,” Simon said fearfully.

He understood all right. He knew the penalty of speaking against the Deacon. Besides to whom would he speak? Who would believe him?

“Bring me my night cap. I don’t need you to rub me tonight the pain has subsided, but you can share the cocoa as usual.”

“Ok, Sir. Thank you, Sir,” Simon said, thankful that the torture was now over.

He escaped through the door and went to get the flask. That night was the beginning of many nights and days and years of pain and suffering, and a realisation that he could do nothing about what was happening to him. The Deacon never failed to remind him how lucky he was that he had taken him in to live with him.

“No one wanted you, remember that,” he would say to him, whenever he seemed reluctant to do as he had asked. He was right. He had nowhere to go. None of his relatives had responded to his letters. Where would he live? Sometimes the sessions would leave Simon crying. The Deacons’ fondling caused extreme pain.

At times, it was torturous. He became whatever the Deacon wanted him to be. He did whatever the Deacon wanted him to do. He knew he could not tell anyone about what he was going through, because the Deacon was an important person in the community. He was trapped and, therefore, obliged to tolerate what he later learnt was physical and sexual abuse.

32

Emotional turmoil

Simon was experiencing many conflicting emotions. He felt anger and disgust towards the Deacon and at himself, because he caused the problem. He felt sad because someone he trusted betrayed him. He felt alone in his experience...one that he could not disclose to anyone. He felt ashamed because his body was now responding to the Deacon's advances, and he was even beginning to get jealous of what he perceived to be the relationship developing between the Deacon and Henry. Most of all, he felt guilty that he didn't have the power, or the will to stop the Deacon.

Simon knew, after he seen the look of fear in Henry's eyes, that the Deacon was sexually abusing him. Simon blamed himself for what he was happening to Henry, because he has kept the

Deacon's secret for the past four years and thus allowed him to prey on others.

"This must stop," he whispered.

He planned to speak to the Deacon that night. He knew from the look and the Deacon's reaction that he would be reprimanded for what happened on the veranda between him and Henry. At that moment, however, he didn't care. Maybe he would regret it later, but he knew that he had to take a stand.

Simon rehearsed his chosen words carefully and waited patiently for the Deacon's appearance at the kitchen door. He didn't appear within an hour and Simon could hear the sound of the piano from the living room.

Good, Simon thought, *perhaps he's not ready to face me either*.

He went into his bedroom to complete the assignment for his class. He had just completed this when the piano stopped suddenly, and he heard the Deacon scream his name.

Panic engulfed Simon when he heard the Deacon scream. He rushed to the living room. From the door, he saw the Deacon lying prostrate on his back breathing heavily, with a man standing over him muttering to himself.

"What's the matter?" Simon asked terrified.

He gingerly took a step towards them. He stopped. The unknown man had turned to look at him and was walking slowly towards him. Simon saw the dripping knife. They looked at each other. Neither said a word. Simon thought it was his turn to die because he was certain that the Deacon was already dead. His heart began to beat more rapidly, and he could feel his body shaking. He tried to run, but his body would not co-operate. His legs felt like lead. He tried speaking but nothing came out.

Simon recognized the man as Teddy, Mrs Clarke's grandson, who had disappeared some two years previously. Everyone had said that he was 'not right in the head'. He had been the Deacon's gardener and something had happened between him and the Deacon. After that, he disappeared from the district.

He walked up to Simon, stretched out the hand that held the knife and said, "I did it for you. He can't harm you now. No more," and shook his head.

Teddy was trembling; his eyes were glazed. He was sweating profusely. Simon took the knife without thinking. Teddy appeared to be in a daze as he continued to walk slowly out of the house. He kept muttering to himself, repeating the same words.

"No more will get hurt."

Simon watched him open the door and walk down the steps.

The whole incident took no more than two minutes, but for Simon it was a lifetime. He looked down at his hand now holding the bloodied knife. He screamed as he looked at his now bloodied hand. He dropped the knife in a panic and wiped his hand on his clothes. He wanted to move closer to the Deacon but his feet would not let him. From where he stood, he could see that the Deacon was still breathing, but it was irregular. He could see that the Deacon had been stabbed in the chest because of the bloodstain on his shirt. He was terrified to go closer, and his legs were shaking uncontrollably.

History repeating itself, he thought.

Simon had discovered his mother in much the same way. All the awful memories associated with that now began to resurface. Someone had broken into their house; she had tried to stop him and was stabbed and left to die. Those memories now overwhelmed Simon and he began to grieve for his mother all over again. He began to cry quietly before it turned to howling. Simon lost all sense of time and space. He didn't hear the knock on the open door and the footsteps of Mr Small, the neighbour entering the house.

Mr Small saw Simon kneeling over the Deacon, crying and babbling inaudible words. He took in the scene immediately.

"Oh! My God what happened here?" he asked and rushed over to the Deacon's side.

"Pull yourself together Simon," Mr Small screamed looking directly at him.

"Did you do this?"

He quickly realized that Simon was incoherent. "Oh, my God! Oh, my God!" He repeated.

He busied himself with the Deacon. He checked for a pulse, and to see if he was still breathing, but the Deacon didn't respond.

"My God!" he exclaimed once more and turned to look at Simon.

"I think it's too late? I'll have to call the police." He walked over to the table to use the telephone.

"Police!" Simon enquired in a confused tone. "Police! Why?"

"You killed the Deacon," Mr Small replied turning to look at him.

"I'm so sorry," Simon kept muttering. He had not shifted from his kneeling position next to the Deacon. He rocked backwards and forwards staring straight ahead.

Simon looked a mess with tears streaming down his face and his clothes bloodied from the knife. He would gaze down at the body of the Deacon from time to time. Each time he did he would begin to wail. He could not compose himself. He swung between restless calm and hysterical outbursts and that is how the police found him.

At the station, they could not make any sense of what he was saying. He appeared to be confusing the death of the Deacon with that of his mother. He continued to deny killing the Deacon and continued to mutter that Teddy had been the murderer, not only of the Deacon, but also of his mother.

After some hours, the police decided to let Simon get some rest and to continue the interrogation their next morning.

They released Simon at noon the next day. They told him that they had found Teddy Clarke and that he had admitted killing the Deacon to save him.

33

Back to the beginning

"Well! Well!" Sandra said when Martha was finished. He couldn't be her son. Never. He was disgusting. He was perverted. Where did he learn about all that kind of nastiness?"

Martha placed her hand in Sandra's.

"Stop berating yourself, girl, No one can hold you responsible for that. The last time you saw him he was a tiny baby. It has to be something he learnt."

"Yes, that's what Brendon told me."

Sandra had met Brendon again, but this time it was at her house. By then he had heard from the police the circumstances that led to the death of his son. He had been distraught and blamed himself for not being firm enough with Jason when he initially saw the signs.

Mary had taken ill when Jason was twelve. Brendon could not cope with both him and Mary so Jason was sent to boarding school. However, before he left to attend the school, Mary insisted that they should tell him that he had been adopted. They explained that they had wanted to give him a better life than he would have had on the island. He accepted their explanation and thanked them for saving him.

Mary died five years later. Jason took his adoptive mother's death very badly. What Brendon didn't know at the time was that Mary had left a letter for Jason to have after she died. In this letter she explained that Brendon was Jason's real father. She hoped that this would bring them closer. However, the information made Jason even more curious about his real mother. When he asked Brendon who his mother was, Brendon had refused to tell him. Their relationship changed for the worse thereafter.

Two weeks after his seventeenth birthday, Brendon walked into Jason's bedroom one night and found him and another boy, who was spending the night in the same bed, doing what he termed something 'ungodly'. He asked the boy to leave the house straight away and Jason insisted on leaving with the boy, after informing Brendon that he would not be returning to the house after his studies, but would be joining the priesthood. Brendon could have stopped paying his college fees, but didn't feel that that would help. So instead, he contacted the principal informing him of what had happened.

The principal assured him that he would deal with the matter and Brendon thought no more about it. Especially, as he had been assured by the Principal that, "boys sometimes go through these phases of experimentation". Jason never returned to his house, however. Brendon would hear from him about his exploits in Africa, South America, and the Caribbean. Jason had spoken to Brendon just a few weeks before his murder. He had said that he was planning on coming to England for two weeks and that he wanted to meet him. The next contact Brendon had had was the phone call from the police. He would therefore be taking Jason's body back to England to be laid next to his adoptive mother's.

"And that's the end of that?" asked Martha, a sly grin on her face.

"He was my 'once upon a time' man," Sandra replied looking across the horizon sadly.

"And, what about Thomas, surely it would be nice to see him again."

"Yes it would." Sandra replied.

He and Maureen seemed to get on well, but Sandra had instructed Maureen her not to speak about him in her presence and Maureen had obliged.

Sandra and Martha were sitting on the same side of the picnic bench facing the ocean. They were on the ridge once again, but the rock that they used to sit on was no longer there.

Instead the area had been smoothed off and the rock replaced by picnic tables. A bandstand had also been erected and the cluster of houses where Sandra had lived no longer existed either. The area had been turned into a huge park and in between the casuarinas, flamboyant palm and grape trees were picnic tables and benches. Most Sundays, afternoon concerts were held here.

Even though some things had changed over the years, this was still their favourite spot. Looking over from their bench, the semi-circle was no longer as well-defined as it had been when they were children and there were now four six-storey buildings on the strip. Much of the street was hidden by these buildings.

These new properties housed apartments, places of entertainment, stores selling food, clothes and hardware to the public, together with the rum shops and those specialty shops selling local artefacts to tourists. The church was still there. It had not changed. It looked as if time had stood still. Today two tourist ships had docked in the deep-water harbour. These boats looked nothing like the ones which Sandra and Martha had seen when they were growing up. These were huge with between three and four thousand passengers on each one.

Friday and Saturday nights remained the favourite time for a visit to the strip for visitors and locals. Only now the food on offer was more varied, exotic and foreign, with pizzas, rotis, wraps, kebabs, and chips reflecting the changing population.

Martha and Sandra usually met here twice a month to reminisce and to discuss current affairs. However, today their minds were on one thing only. After describing Simon's life with the Deacon, Martha turned to her attention to talk about her grandson, Teddy. She was able to get a lawyer for him. The lawyer was working hard to get him sent back to the home while psychiatric reports were completed. They were still waiting for the result of these.

Two people were approaching them from the side of the bandstand. Sandra recognized her daughter immediately; the other was a stout elderly looking man, whose head gleamed in early afternoon sunlight. They were walking systematically as if they were on parade.

Martha was the first to speak.

"For an old man, he's as sprightly as ever." She said with a smile.

"Who?" Sandra asked.

"Stop pretending," Martha replied and slapped her on the leg.

Yes, she was pretending, because she could not believe her eyes. He still had that boyish look and broad shoulders. He used to be likened to Muhammad Ali, and he had retained the look. Suddenly he was in front of her with one hand outstretched.

"Hello Sandra," he said in a strong 'British Caribbean accent'.

She looked at the outstretched hand. It was sweaty and shook nervously. She then looked up at the face of the man, now smiling down at her.

Over the years, she had rehearsed so many different things to say to him if she was ever to meet him again. However, now not one of them came to mind. Instead her lips trembled. She stood, slapped his hand away and pushed him in the chest.

"Fuck you, fuck you, fuck you," she screamed at him.

He grabbed both her hands and pulled her towards him. He wrapped his arms around her saying, "Sssshhhh, Sssshhhhhh, I know and I am so sorry."

Two hours later, Thomas and Sandra were sitting in one of the new restaurants on the Strip. Maureen and Martha had left them to catch up on sixty years of news. Sandra heard that Thomas's father had told Thomas that Sandra had moved on with her life and was not interested in him anymore. He had been hurt and had wanted to hurt her also, so he had written to say that he was getting married. However, this didn't actually happen until years later and then it didn't last very long, because his mind was always on her and the daughter, whom he had never seen. He had two other children and four grandchildren. They had never been to the island. He was not too sure if they wanted to.

Thomas had returned with his father. He was thinking about coming back for good but he had not decided yet. He was busy trying to find the right house to buy.

Three people were sitting on the picnic table eyes firmly fixed on the street below and its environs. They were very animated in their conversation.

On the table were a picnic basket and an ice bucket with a bottle of champagne. It was the last week of summer and some boys and girls were diving off the cliff.

"Haven't things changed," Sandra observed. "At one time you would not find any girls, now they've taken over."

"True, true," both Martha and Thomas said in unison.

Only one ship was in today; they could see the tourists streaming off, and descending into taxis and private cars for hire situated on the beach.

"I've been promised a cruise by my son," Martha announced. "I hope I manage to take it before I die."

"Ladies, it's time for the champagne," Thomas changed the subject.

He got up and within a minute had popped the cork and filled the three glasses on the table. They raised their glasses.

Thomas said, "To true friends, those are have gone ahead and those who are still with us. I salute you ladies."

"Hear, hear," said both Martha and Sandra together. They clinked glasses.

As the sun dipped into the ocean, three people with their heads close together, sat on the picnic bench closest to the ridge overlooking 'The Strip'. They had been here since the early hours of the morning. When they were tired, they took breaks on sleeping bags they had brought with them. Their children, grand children and great grand children checked on them from time. They and the curious onlookers thought they were crazy. None of them would know that these three were catching up on the past sixty years of their lives.

34

New beginnings

Two weeks after the murder of the Deacon, much had been revealed. Some details were public knowledge, whilst those who were personally involved had additional information.

The police had discovered that the Deacon had been seducing young boys over twenty years. When complaints arose the church moved him to another area of the world. He had skilfully manipulated the children into participating in the disgusting behaviour. Then to ensure their continued compliance, he had used bribes, threats, and force.

Three such persons were Simon, Teddy, and Peter. They had been living with the fear of retribution and abandonment, and feelings of complicity, embarrassment, guilt and shame. All these conspired to silence them and inhibit their disclosures of abuse.

The specialist disclosed to Peter Preston and his family, at their first session the gradual grooming process that Henry would have gone through. He begged the family not to blame themselves for what had happened, they didn't cause it, but instead he asked them to continue to show Henry that they loved him.

Peter said, "At least now, he won't be able to harm anyone else."

Peter had already decided what the family would do after these sessions with the specialist although he had not yet discussed the plans with Sally.

Recently Sally had been asking questions about his strange behaviour. She had waited up for him the night he had gone to see Trina. She must have noticed the bruises on his forehead, but had said nothing. All she had asked when he entered the house, was if he was all right. He had replied by shaking his head and had gone straight into the bathroom.

Peter had not heard from Trina for two weeks. He thought that she was still vexed about their last encounter. He had left a letter for her at the office that last day explaining that he was taking leave to deal with family problems. This was not like her. He needed to see her. She needed to know about his plans. However, he didn't want to go to the apartment. He needed to meet her at some neutral place. He dialled her cell number again. She didn't answer and it went to message centre. He didn't want to leave a message.

Two hours later, in the middle of the family dinner, his phone rang. Sally looked at him daring him to answer. It was a long-standing family rule that cell phones were not answered during the dinner. Peter normally had his turned off. He checked the number looked at Sally and said. "This is urgent, I must take it," and walked into the bedroom. He had just finished arranging to meet Trina, when she walked into the bedroom.

"Can I ask you a question, Peter?" she said softly.

"Why not?" Peter replied irritated.

"Are you having an affair?" He turned to her sharply.

"Yes, and what about you?"

"No, no," she replied shocked. "I could smell her on you last Tuesday night." She raised her voice. "So, what now? What is going to happen to our family?"

"I think you need to keep your voice down," he replied calmly and headed for the shower.

"You can't go; I think we need to speak about this."

"Yes, we need to speak about it, but not now, later. I have an important appointment."

Sally was livid. How dare he speak to her as if

she was a child? He was the one who had just admitted to having an affair. She needed to know what was going to become of her and their family. She just couldn't understand what had got into him these two weeks. He was like a stranger, not the man she had married.

Peter met Trina as planned. He picked her up from her apartment and took her to the cove, a twenty-minute drive out of town. Trina was very subdued.

"How's work," Peter asked trying to break the ice.

"Good," she replied soberly. They remained quiet for some minutes and then Peter began to speak. He apologized for what had happened. He explained how the murder of Deacon had affected his family and in particular his son, and how conflicted his mind had been that evening, especially as earlier that day she had informed him that the Deacon was his uncle. Trina was sobbing even before he had finished. He had never before heard her cry. "I didn't know. I didn't know," she sobbed. He took out his handkerchief and gave it to her to clean herself up. "My grandmother said he was a wicked man, but I didn't understand. I'm so sorry," she said and placed her hand on his thigh and squeezed it. He looked ahead of him and continued to speak. "For the sake of my son I have to move away from here."

"No, no, you can't."

"Trina, don't pretend, you'll just replace me with someone else," he said calmly looking at her.

"Maybe, but I'll miss you. What about my job?"

"Your job will be secure; you don't need to worry about that." Peter dropped Trina off back to her apartment with the promise of seeing her again before he left for the holiday with his family, but now he had one more task to perform. He drove to Wendy's house and parked, walked up to her door which opened as he was about to knock on it.

"Come in, come in," said Wendy smiling. She was glad to hear from Peter.

She smells good, Peter thought. Peter stepped into her tiny apartment. Not much had changed since the last time he had been here, except she had added an extra painting. It made the wall look unbalanced.

"Sit down, sit down, Can I make you some tea, or would you prefer wine?"

"Tea, please," he answered apprehensively. He remembered what had happened the last time she had offered him wine. Wendy looked disappointed. She busied herself lighting the stove and getting the cups for the tea. The kettle boiled quickly and as poured water into the two cups containing the teabags. She asked. "So what's new? Milk and sugar?"

Peter shook his head. She brought the two cups on a tray to the table where he was sitting. "Thank you, Peter said. "Well to answer your question. Plenty is new." He once again related the story about the Deacon's premature death and his family connection.

"So you're going to leave and the 'affair' what will happen to that?" she asked. Peter was horrified at her response, but decided to keep his cool. He replied calmly.

"That too is finished. It was finished long before."

"Oh," said Wendy, looking disappointed. Peter left her half an hour later. She was still hoping that they could at least have sex together even if there was nothing in it for him. Peter thought that she must be a lonely and desperate woman.

He and his wife spoke late into the night. He knew that their relationship would have changed forever. He could not promise that he would never again have an affair because he still had very strong feelings for Trina. He might be tempted again, and he knew that she would be willing. The next morning he was up early. He turned to his wife, kissed her on the forehead, and said. "Come, let's go, and speak to the children about the holiday, and the other plans we have made."

"That's a big one, Henry," Peter announced

excitedly, looking at the size of the fish that Henry was struggling to reel in. “Let me help you.” It was late evening and Peter and his two sons were fishing off the rocks. This was the first time that Henry had caught anything of significance. Usually he would watch his older brother and father with envy as they reeled in their catch from the bridge. Tonight was his night.

This was their second holiday in this part of the island. It had been Henry’s suggestion that they took a camping holiday. His mother had been against it initially, but one look from his Dad and her views changed. Camping was better because he could bring his two dogs along with him. His father had brought him another puppy ‘to keep Pip’s company’ his father had said. His mother was only staying one week. She had to get back to the new restaurant that she now managed. He was glad because he would be able to play with his dogs more freely than if she was there. He would not have to watch her cringe every time he frolicked with them.

This was the happiest Peter had seen his son in a long time. He walked with him to the bank of the river and helped him clean the fish. Henry looked up at his father and smiled widely as they continued to delve into his first real catch. Things had changed since those dark days. Peter had moved his family to another town. Churches and schools were changed and they set up franchises of their restaurant. Sally managed one and Peter the other. They also employed relief managers, so that they could spend time with their family, and take more holidays with them. The psychologist had suggested that this was the best thing to do to save their son. They were right, because presently there was a lot of laughter in the family

Henry's relationship with his parents and siblings was better than ever, and he was excelling once again in school and sports. The family continued to be counselled and Henry, in particular, as despondency could sometimes set in.

Peter now kept a closer eye on what both of his sons were up to, where they went, with whom, and whom they met when they got there. Sometimes, they would become irritated with the questions. However, he would make no excuses for the new attitude he had adopted in order to keep his family safe from predators.

BOOKS BY THE SAME AUTHOR

www.ingramcontent.com/pod-product-compliance
Lightning Source LLC
Chambersburg PA
CBHW071306170626
46809CB00001B/348

* 9 7 8 9 7 6 9 5 5 6 7 0 6 *